PRAISE

"...the book is enriched by the author's cleverly phrased prose and convincing characterization. The surprise ending will satisfy and delight many mystery fans. A diverting mystery that offers laughs and chills." -*Kirkus Reviews*

"An impressive cozy mystery from a promising author." -*Mystery Tribune*

"A really funny mystery with a chicklit feel." -Susan M. Boyer, USA Today Bestselling Author of *Lowcountry Bordello*

"Designer Dirty Laundry shows that even the toughest crime is no match for a sleuth in fishnet stockings who knows her way around the designer department. A delightful debut." -Kris Neri, Lefty Award-Nominated author of *Revenge For Old Times' Sake*

"Combining fashion and fatalities, Diane Vallere pens a winning debut mystery...a sleek and stylish read." -Ellen Byerrum, National Bestselling author of the Crime of Fashion mysteries

"Vallere once again brings her knowledgeable fashion skills to the forefront, along with comedy, mystery, and a saucy romance. *Buyer, Beware* did not disappoint!" *-Chick Lit Plus*

"Fashion is always at the forefront, but never at the cost of excellent writing, humorous dialogue, or a compelling story." *-Kings River Life*

"A captivating new mystery voice, Vallere has stitched together haute couture and murder in a stylish mystery. Dirty Laundry has never been so engrossing!" -Krista Davis, *New York Times* Bestselling Author of The Domestic Diva Mysteries

"Samantha Kidd is an engaging amateur sleuth." *-Mysterious Reviews*

"It keeps you at the edge of your seat. I love the description of clothes in this book...if you love fashion, pick this up!" *-Los Angeles Mamma Blog*

"Diane Vallere takes the reader through this cozy mystery with her signature wit and humor." -Mary Marks, *NY Journal of Books*

"...be careful; you might just laugh right out loud as you read." -3 no 7 Looks at Books

A SAMANTHA KIDD MYSTERY

FAHRENHEIT 501

Book 12 in the Samantha Kidd Mystery Series

A Polyester Press Mystery

e-ISBN: 9781954579262

paperback print ISBN: 9781954579309

hardcover print ISBN: 9781954579354

A SAMANTHA KIDD MYSTERY

FAHRENHEIT 501

DIANE VALLERE

Polyester Press

For the cult of denim

LESS THAN AUSPICIOUS ARRIVAL

"Dress appropriately," the invitation advised. Considering the invitation was for membership in a secret fashion society that I hadn't known existed until I picked up last week's mail, the definition of "appropriately" had more layers than the sweater shelf in my closet. These were my people, and I wanted them to accept me as one of them.

The secret fashion society called themselves the Fahrenheit Guild. Aside from the dress code and address, there wasn't anything on the invitation to tell me much about them, so I'd turned my attention to the internet, where I'd found the phrase "secret fashion society." I had to give them credit; they appeared to take the secret part seriously.

When my research about the guild didn't net much, I'd turned my investigative talents toward the castle. I mean, why was there a castle in the middle of Ribbon, Pennsylvania?

The imposing stone structure in front of me had been

built in the twenties by a German immigrant. Instead of the expected architecture of a Holy Grail-era castle, Brae-burn Castle was a two-story edifice modeled after one in Bavaria. The castle keep was on the left, standing easily twice as tall as the rest of the building. Constructed of local materials and built by regional craftsmen, the castle was a testament to what the city of Ribbon was like during pre-World War II times. I loved these unexpected structures. They reminded me my town had a rich history that existed long before I was born.

After trying on half my wardrobe, I'd settled on a vintage Bonnie Cashin skirt suit. I smoothed the jacket and tapped the heavy iron knocker against the wooden door. The invitation said I would be greeted at the entrance, so I waited with the crisp chill of an October evening snaking around my legs. The more I followed the instructions from the Fahrenheit Guild, the more I felt like Alice falling down the rabbit hole. For the briefest moment, I wondered if I should have commissioned a blue dress with white pinafore instead.

The door opened by a man who appeared to be a hundred and five. "Ms. Kidd, I presume?" he asked. He wore a black tuxedo, which I dismissed as a uniform for staff. He seemed unimpressed by my ensemble.

"Yes. I'm Samantha Kidd." I reached into my handbag for my invitation, but he waved it away.

"The others are waiting in the clubroom at the end of the hall." He turned his back to me and walked away.

"Wait," I said. I pushed the invitation back into the depths of my handbag and reached out. The man turned back. I didn't grab him, but my hand was headed toward his arm, and his eyes took in the possibility of contact with what appeared to be dismay. Slowly, I retracted my hand and pretended I'd made a perfectly acceptable gesture. "Can you tell me anything about them?" I asked. "The guild," I added for clarification. "I assume they meet here regularly. I couldn't find anything on the internet, but I guess that's what makes them secret. What are they like to work for?" I smiled, hoping the elderly man would find me charming. (So far, nothing.) I lowered my voice. "Are they at least good tippers?"

"Follow me." He turned and walked through a dark hallway made of exposed brick walls and ceiling. The man's footsteps were silent on faded and worn overlapping Turkish rugs that appeared to have been there since the place was built. I scampered into the hallway to keep up with him, and the rubber tip of my heel caught in the rug. I bent to free it, noticing the carpet's threadbare condition. The man turned, and I smiled, slipped my foot back into my shoe, and walked on my tiptoes the rest of the way.

I wanted to ask him to slow down, but I sensed I'd already done something wrong, and I didn't want to compound my social gaffe. The hallway was poorly lit, and the man's black tux made his figure harder to track. Eventually, I reached a heavy wooden door not unlike the entrance. The door was slowly closing, and my powers of deduction told me it couldn't close without having been open first, so I took a calculated risk and yanked on the handle. It swung toward me easier than I'd expected, and I had to step back to avoid being hit. Inside was a room filled with the best-dressed people I'd ever seen in Ribbon, Pennsylvania.

"Ladies and Gentlemen of the Fahrenheit Guild, I'd

like to introduce Samantha Kidd," the butler said. "Though after her less-than-auspicious arrival, I may rethink the nomination of her as my successor."

Successor? I thought this man worked here. Was this a job interview?

Did I ask him about tips?

My eyes had finally adjusted to the dim light in the room and I studied the man. I'd misjudged his age; up close he didn't look a day over ninety-nine. He was about my height, and the lines of his tux offset the curvature of his spine. His eyebrows were drawn low over his eyes, indicating dissatisfaction. I'd like to say I knew what I'd done wrong, but I can be blissfully ignorant when it comes to my personal behavior.

A petite woman in a black St. John knit suit stood. "Hans, we've been through this." She shifted her attention to me. "Welcome, Samantha." She smiled warmly, and I smiled back.

"Thank you," I said. "I'm delighted to be here. I had no idea—"

The woman held up her hand to shush me, and I stopped talking. Was that another misstep? My smile froze in place, and I looked away from her and at the others. Someone in here would tell me what was going on. I'd approached the castle door feeling like Alice in Wonderland, but now that I was inside, the night felt more like *Eyes Wide Shut*.

The woman approached the front of the room. She was younger than Hans. I'd place her in her late seventies. Her hair was gray in the front and black in the back, cut in a razor-sharp angled bob that graced her angular jawline. Her suit was accessorized with a triple strand of

Jackie-O pearls that filled in the collar, and her earrings appeared to be Paloma Picasso for Tiffany's. (I didn't always identify garments by designer, but I'd been studying as prep for tonight, and it seemed a shame to let the knowledge go to waste.)

"Samantha, I'm Cecile Sézane." She held out her hand and I shook it. "We were finishing some business prior to your interview. Would you mind waiting in the hallway?" She glanced back at Hans, who hadn't dropped the glare from his expression.

"Sure," I said. I turned toward the door and then turned back. "Am I early? The invitation said seven."

"We've been discussing outstanding matters," she offered. She extended her arm toward the door. "I can't invite you to sit in until you've been properly vetted. You *do* understand, don't you?"

"Yes. Of course." I pointed to the door. "I'll wait out here."

The door to the room opened, and a woman entered with a tray. Cecile took it from her and set it on the end of the table. "Marguerite, can you show Samantha out?"

The woman nodded. "Of course," she said. She left the room, and I followed.

"Are they always like this?" I asked.

"Like what?" she asked. I studied her face and wondered if she had no opinion of the group in the clubroom, or if her job depended on her allegiance to them.

I considered my choice of words, but before I discovered a politically-correct term for snobby, Marguerite spoke. "I've heard some heated discussions come from the clubroom when they have meetings. Hans is usually the instigator. But his bark is worse than his bite if you want my opinion." She cocked her head. "You'll do fine." She smiled and then turned away and left through a door farther down the hall.

As the heavy door to the clubroom swung shut behind me, I stepped a few feet into the hallway and rested against a wall. It's not every day you find yourself standing around the interior of a castle, and it appeared as though I was alone. I didn't want to veer too far from the clubroom, but Cecile had asked me to give them privacy, so hovering in eavesdropping range seemed a bad idea. (The possibility that they were talking about me made it a tempting option, but this felt like one of those do-the-opposite-of-your-impulse moments.)

I eased my way a few feet down the hallway. A shadow moved on the ground in front of me. A few seconds later, a scruffy cat crossed the hallway and disappeared. I followed the cat to the vestibule and spent the next ten minutes trying to get him to trust me.

"Samantha?" I heard.

The cat ran away. A few seconds later, Cecile approached me. She gestured me toward her. "We're ready for you now."

I made my way back to the clubroom. As I tiptoed over the carpets, this time I heard muffled voices arguing. I passed a room whose door had been closed, and a surreptitious glance showed Hans reprimanding a young, red-haired man. I didn't know the old man well enough to know if his crabby expression was his default, or if the younger man had done something worthy of Hans's criticism, but I didn't like what I saw.

On a whim, I stopped outside the door and poked my head in. "Hans?" I called. The interruption had the desired effect. Hans glared at me. His face was red, brow even more furrowed than it had been upon my arrival. "The guild is ready to resume the meeting. You're coming, aren't you?"

I hovered in the doorway and held my arm out in the direction of the clubroom. I forced a bright smile onto my face and maintained eye contact.

Eventually, Hans turned back to the boy, raised his cane, and shook it at him. "Watch yourself, or you'll be next." He put his cane back down and left the room, pausing next to me. "And *you* need to learn to mind your own business." He raised his cane to waist-height and used it to push me back against the door. "One more strike and you're out too."

2

BROWN BOUCLE AFTER EIGHT

I STARED AT HANS'S BACK AS HE RETURNED TO THE clubroom, and then turned to the younger man. His head was still down, and he didn't look at me. "Crisis averted," I said in a friendly tone of voice.

The young man looked up at me. There was a red mark on his cheekbone, visible above his facial scruff. I entered the room and approached him. "Did he hit you?"

He stepped back and put both hands up. "Just leave me alone, will you?" he said. "I don't want to get into any more trouble."

My Achilles heel was helping people, and in most cases, the recipients of my help didn't want it. Now that I was somewhat self-aware, it was easier to recognize the trigger. The truth was, I don't know what I'd seen while passing the room, and for all I knew, Hans had every reason to reprimand the guy.

Underdogs, though, were my second Achilles heel, probably because I saw them as kindred spirits.

I returned to the meeting. Half of the original group

was gone, and this time a row of six chairs had been lined up behind a table facing the front of the room. We'd gone from *Eyes Wide Shut* to the audition scene in *Flashdance*.

Cecile closed the door and took a seat. A near-empty pitcher of water sat on a silver tray in the center of the table, and six glasses in various stages of full to empty sat in front of each seat.

Hans sat in a chair farthest from the door. Between him and the seat Cecile chose were a zaftig woman with bouncy blond hair dressed in a man's dress shirt tucked into a black satin skirt, and a thin man in an embroidered western-style shirt paired with black tuxedo pants. On the other side of Cecile was an Asian woman. Her jet-black hair was pulled back into a ponytail and her forehead was covered in blunt-cut bangs. She wore a flowy silk kimono printed with pink cherry blossoms paired with an ivory silk tank top and matching silk trousers. A vacant seat was between the Asian woman and the door, and a notepad, pen, and water glass occupied the table.

"Samantha," Cecile started, "Allow me to introduce us." She turned to her right and leaned forward. "You've already met Hans. Next to him is Lucy, and this is Buck." The man in the embroidered shirt raised his glass, tipped it in my direction, and took a drink. Cecile turned to her left. "This is Ahn." Each of the members smiled and nodded in turn. I immediately decided my first order of business, after being voted in, was to suggest nametags, because this many names in this short amount of time was a recipe for disaster.

Cecile continued. "Tonight's interview is a formality. We call it an interview, but we'd like to get to know you as much as we want you to get to know us."

"That's great," I said, feeling the adrenaline from my encounter with Hans subside. "I do have questions. How long have you been meeting? When did the guild start? How do you keep it a secret?"

"I told you not to tell her it was a formality," Hans said, visibly disgusted. "She thinks she's in. Look at her. Wearing brown after eight." He shook his head in distaste.

I glanced down at my vintage Bonnie Cashin ensemble. It was a skirt suit made of heavily textured brown and ivory boucle trimmed in cognac leather. The skirt had an A-line, and the collar of the jacket was oversized enough to frame out my face. When I'd come across it in the Ribbon hospital resale shop, it had significant damage from an enthusiastic moth. I'd had it repaired and relined at a reweaving shop on the Main Line, and until this moment thought no one would notice.

"I wasn't aware there was a dress code," I said, addressing the group. "The invitation said you're a fashion society, and I thought you would appreciate this choice. Bonnie Cashin *is* widely credited as being the pioneer of American sportswear."

"Is that what you think this is?" Hans asked. "A forum to discuss who you, a non-member, think is an important contributor to American fashion?"

Heat rose over my cheeks. "I don't know what this is," I said. I quickly scanned the rest of the faces watching me and then directed my reply to Hans. "I received an invitation to join your club, which I— perhaps mistakenly—thought meant someone here thought I had something to contribute." I tore my gaze from Hans's crabby face and one by one looked each of the people seated at the table in the eye. "If that's not why I'm here, then could someone please enlighten me to the real reason?"

Buck, the man in the western shirt pulled a silver flask out of his shirt pocket and unscrewed the cap, then refilled his crystal tumbler with something amber. He capped the flask and tucked it away, then raised his glass in my direction. "She holds up under interrogation, I'll give her that," he said to Lucy. He drained his glass and set it on the table.

Lucy grinned at me. The two of them, closest in age to me, provided more of a welcoming vibe than I'd felt all evening, and I allowed a shy smile in return. I was teetering on the edge of overwhelm, trying to come up with mnemonic tricks to remember their names, when Cecile spoke again.

"What other questions do you have for us?"

"What exactly *is* the Fahrenheit Guild?"

"We're fashion historians," Cecile said. She gestured to include the others at the table. "Each of us represents an important fashion pattern. We memorize the components of a garment, the design details, and the historical context of them."

"How does that work?" I asked. "Where do you get the patterns? Are there archives here? Do you host exhibits? Do the design houses know about you?"

Buck leaned back and draped his arms over the chair. "Once a garment is nominated, we debate the merits of it. Is it already a classic? Is it destined to become one? Who has it influenced? How long has it been around? Can we trace the history to a moment in time, or was it the hallmark of a designer's career?"

"Like jersey dresses and Halston?" I asked.

"Exactly," Lucy answered. "We vote to approve a garment then use club dues to purchase two versions of the same thing. One goes into the archives and the other gets deconstructed. That becomes the pattern."

"You take apart a classic garment to make a pattern," I said, slowly processing what that meant. To most people, it would have sounded like a lot of work for nothing, but to a person steeped in fashion history, it sounded equal parts genius and sacrilege.

"You asked if the design houses knew of us," Cecile said. "Founding members have reached out to them, sometimes successfully, but mostly not. More and more we're faced with designers who want to free themselves from what they've once stood for, so they can shift into new directions and capture a younger audience. Our goals of equating them with one pattern are at odds with their business strategies."

Lucy leaned forward and looked at the others. "Remember when the people at Pucci wanted to stop making prints?" Several of the panelists snickered.

Cecile continued. "We're not concerned with business growth. We care about the preservation of history."

Lucy interjected, "There have been attempts to shut us down."

It sounded like make-believe, even to a person like me. Why would anyone care if a group of people in a mid-sized town sixty miles west of Philadelphia wanted to deconstruct old garments and memorize them for some perceived noble motivation? I felt like I was being put on. Like a camera crew was going to pop out from behind a secret wall at any moment and shout "Gotcha!"

But as I scanned the faces in front of me, I saw nothing

that told me this was a joke. Cecile took the group seriously, and Hans looked as if I alone would bring dishonor to his secret club.

If this was for real and the rest of the members were anything like these five, then I'd found my tribe. My eyes lingered on the empty spot next to Ahn. From where I stood, I could see that notes had been made on the top sheet of the abandoned notepad, but it was impossible to read them.

My attention was pulled away from the notepad when Cecile asked me a question about my background. I'd practiced this response at home with my shoe designer husband, and the answer flowed out smoothly.

"After getting a Bachelor's Degree in the history of fashion, I was hired by Bentley's New York department store," I started. I continued with the highlights: worked up their corporate ladder and moved back to Ribbon with the expectation of working for a legendary fashion figure. This was the part where my "experience" got sticky. A series of homicides, unrelated except for two things: their connection to the world of fashion and me, had dotted the next near-decade, giving the term "crimes of fashion" new meaning. I went with a glossier narrative.

"Since moving to Ribbon, I've mostly worked freelance, always supporting the fashion industry," I wrapped up. I gave them the full wattage of my smile, shooting for something more Tom Cruise than Brittany Spears.

"What do you know about jeans?" Hans asked abruptly.

"Jeans?" I repeated. "I'm not a fan of fast fashion, and designer denim is one of the biggest culprits. Whenever I need space in my closet, jeans are the first to go."

I'd been speaking directly to Hans, but now, I peeked at the others. Ahn made notes, and both Lucy and Buck were staring at Hans. Cecile's gaze fell somewhere around my midsection. Lucy smiled at me, and I welcomed the feeling of kinship. I smiled back.

"If I am to become a member of the Fahrenheit Guild, you'll never see me in jeans," I added. "I may have misinterpreted the dress code tonight, but that won't happen again."

I'd always felt like owning up to your errors made more sense than pretending you hadn't made them, and in this case, my brown-boucle-after-eight, regardless of its provenance, had already been made an issue. There was something about Hans's line of questions that hinted at an agenda, and if I were to be his successor, then he was the one I had to impress.

While I stood at the front of the room, the door opened and Marguerite returned with a fresh pitcher of water. The room remained silent as she moved along the table, refilling Hans's glass, passing by Buck's, and topping off Lucy's. Cecile held her hand over the top of hers and shook her head. Marguerite picked up the empty pitcher and left the new one in its place. As she left, I pointed to the untouched glass next to Ahn. "May I?" I asked.

"Help yourself," Cecile said.

I approached the table and picked up the glass. The ice cubes had melted, making it easy to drink. I drained the glass to quench my thirst and then realized the water had a faint aftertaste. I lowered the glass and peered at the contents. "What is this?" I asked.

"Water," Cecile said. Her voice sounded tinny and far away, and as I turned my head to look at her, I swayed.

Her outline—all their outlines—was hazy, like how people look after you've been swimming in chlorinated water without goggles. I blinked a few times and put my hand out to steady myself with the table. My arms felt heavy, and my legs felt like noodles. I tried to speak, but my mouth had a difficult time forming words. I tried to point to the glass but my arms felt like they'd been weighed down with fifty-pound weights.

"She doesn't look well," someone said, and someone else agreed. Their voices stretched into syllables that were barely decipherable. I needed to sit, but there were no chairs on my side of the table. I dropped to the carpet and then laid back with my arms out on either side. I felt as if I were going to leave a dent in the floor.

I didn't know how, and I didn't know why, but the last thing I thought before closing my eyes was that I was pretty sure I'd just been drugged.

3

HIGHER POWER SPANX

WHEN I OPENED MY EYES, I WAS LYING ON THE LEATHER sofa in the study. Stacks of jeans that had been strewn across it now lay on the floor. My jacket was draped over the top of my handbag, which sat on the floor a few feet away. My silk shell was untucked, and the thick Lycra of my beige Higher Power Spanx was visible. I briefly wondered how that would factor into the Fahrenheit Guild's assessment of my worthiness.

I sat up. The movement felt natural, though the memory of how I'd felt after drinking the water came back. The room was dark, so I switched on the Tiffany lamp and found a clock. It was after ten; I'd been at the castle for less than three hours.

Regardless of my less-than-auspicious interview, it didn't seem possible that the five members of the vetting panel had abandoned me in the messy storage room and left for the night, so I tucked in my shirt, pulled on my jacket, and slipped on my shoes. The hallway was quiet and the clubroom was locked. I crept in the other direction and found Lucy and Buck in the bar.

"Samantha," Lucy announced loudly. "You're awake." She slid off a leather wingback chair and came over to me. "We were all worried. Did you forget to eat today?"

"The water," I said. "It wasn't water."

She looked at Buck and back at me. "Nobody else had a problem. You must have been exhausted. Or maybe it was the stress of the interview? God, when I had my interview, I popped diet pills for a week while I studied. The first thing I did after being accepted was to eat a Big Mac." She held out her hand. "In case you forgot, I'm Lucy. Brooks Brothers shirt."

"That's quite a name."

She laughed. "Lucy Francis. My pattern is the classic Brooks Brothers pinpoint oxford."

"I thought you weren't supposed to tell me what pattern you represented," I said.

"You're pretty much in. Besides, Buck and I don't have the same respect for the rules as the older members." The two of them chuckled.

I shook her hand. Her wrist was covered in thin gold bangles, some dotted with diamonds. They tinkled against each other. I hadn't heard them earlier, but now it seemed like it would have been a difficult sound to mask. "I took them off for the panel," she said, running her hand over them. "They can attract unnecessary attention."

"What happened?" I asked. "to me," I added.

"You collapsed," Lucy said. "It was like you got too heavy to hold yourself up and you laid down on the floor. Nobody has ever done that before, not even the guy we voted out." She raised her glass of bourbon in my direction. "You're going to be fun."

I looked at Buck. He'd been suspiciously silent since I walked in, and that made me uncomfortable. "Is that what you saw?"

He shrugged. "You were stressed. Chicks have a hard time with pressure." He drank from his bourbon glass and kept his eyes on me. His comment felt too inappropriate not to have been bait, and I chose not to give him the satisfaction of a response.

"How did you handle your interview?" I asked him.

"Buck didn't have an interview," Lucy said. "He's a legacy."

I turned to him. "What kind of a name is Buck?"

"Family name. Buckley Owen Hollinger."

"The fourth," Lucy added.

"It's good for one thing: my trust fund."

"Yes, but your nickname is good for limericks," Lucy said.

I'd place Lucy in her mid-fifties, though the faint presence of Botox injection punctures on her forehead suggested she wanted to appear younger. Her body was solid, neither thin nor fat, but somewhere in the middle sizes that are often the hardest to dress. Her skin tone had a pinkish flush, though that may have been due to the bourbon.

Buck, on the other hand, looked like he'd taken style cues from Jeff Goldblum's Apartments.com commercials. His hair was parted on the side and his square black glasses seemed more accessory than a necessity. A vintage Hamilton watch peeked out from under his sleeve. Interesting. I would have picked a fourth-generation legacy candidate for a Patek Philippe.

Buck finished his drink and went to the bar for a refill. I watched him help himself to the contents of a cut crystal decanter, replace the lid, and leave the decanter sitting on the polished maple bar. He didn't seem concerned with the concept of hiding his actions from the staff.

"Where are the others?" I asked Lucy.

"Ahn wasn't feeling well, so she left. Buck and I moved you to the storage room, and Cecile and Hans went to the office to discuss your candidacy," Lucy said. "But don't worry about that. Even if Hans digs in his heels, it'll be four against one. You're as good as in."

"What about the staff?" I asked, thinking of Marguerite and the young man Hans had reprimanded. "Where are they?"

"The staff goes off the clock at nine," Buck said. "We take turns locking the place up on meeting night."

"Whose turn is it tonight?"

"Mine," Buck said while Lucy pointed her finger at him.

Lucy raised her glass a second time, and then, as if recognizing I didn't have a glass, pointed to it. "You want a bourbon?"

I held my hands up and waved off the offer. "No, thanks. I'm not thirsty."

"Thirst has nothing to do with it."

If members of the guild remained at the castle, I didn't feel comfortable leaving, but the longer I stayed, the more I longed for the comfort of my home. For a night that had held so much promise, things had turned eerie. It was frustrating that both Lucy and Buck wrote off my reaction to the water as nerves, but I knew what I'd felt. The problem was, short of peeing in a cup and holding onto the sample, I was metabolizing any evidence that might have existed in my system. Covertly slipping a urine sample into my handbag seemed the kind of thing that would negatively impact my pending application.

"Should we find them?" I asked. "Cecile and Hans. Should we resume the meeting?"

Lucy shook her head. "Too late. Hans starts to fade by nine. If you hadn't pulled your stunt in there, he'd probably be asleep by now."

"It wasn't a stunt," I protested.

"Whether it was or wasn't is immaterial," she said. "You got out of the interview before anybody had a chance to dig into your background."

There was something about the way she said it, the phrase "dig into your background" that said the carefully-crafted answer to their question about my experience wasn't going to go unchecked. I'd been prepared for that. After a profile on me in the local newspaper got picked up by the Associated Press and went national, I was even recognized at the grocery store.

Recently, I'd been involved with a former high school classmate who was imprisoned for murdering her husband. The publicity following that had magnified my reputation. It's one of the reasons I wrote my occasional column for the *Ribbon Eagle* from home while the halo effect of being a do-gooder faded.

Lucy finished her drink and set the empty tumbler on the table. I couldn't shake the feeling that she'd been closely watching me all night. Like Buck's comment about chicks and pressure, hers about my background felt like bait. I didn't know if it was the dim lighting, the creepy castle-setting, or the suspected drugs in my system, but the evening had taken on a hallucinatory edge, and I no longer wanted to stay.

"If you're certain the meeting won't resume, I'm going to leave."

"Sure," Lucy said. "Someone will be in touch regarding your application."

I felt the dismissal in her tone. It was as if by choosing to leave instead of choosing to stay, I'd committed a faux pas that was less forgivable than laying down on the floor in the interview. These people had interesting standards; I'd give them that.

I left the bar and returned to the study to retrieve my handbag. Wilhelm sat on top of a pile of jeans on the sofa. I held out my hand so he could sniff it and then scratched his ears.

He sat still and closed his eyes, achieving the universal cat state of Zen often accompanied by purring. I added my other hand to the scratching routine and took care of both sides of his head and face. He tipped right and left to direct me to different spots, and I stepped closer to get a better angle. My leg brushed against a stack of jeans and they tipped onto the floor, revealing the ashen figure of Hans buried underneath.

4

PEE IN A CUP

No, I THOUGHT. *No, no, no, no, no.*

Not tonight, not now, not here.

Not again.

Wilhelm sensed my energy shift and hopped down from the sofa. There was little doubt that an old man buried under a mound of clothes meant one thing, but I pressed my fingers into the papery flesh on the side of his neck and felt for a pulse.

No pulse.

I pulled my compact out of my handbag and held the mirror in front of his mouth.

No breathing.

Hans had been at the end of his life, but if he'd died by natural causes, he wouldn't be buried under a stack of poorly-folded jeans. That meant this wasn't an accident. And *that* meant I was in a creepy castle with a murderer.

Suddenly, I was afraid to touch anything in the room. I pulled my cell out of my handbag and called nine-one-one. I gave them my name, location, and nature of the emergency all in a hushed voice. I had to tell the others, but the possibility that this had been done by one of them was high, and a warning might light a fuse better left unlit.

There was one thing I could do, one thing I'd thought of earlier that seemed too embarrassing to consider but finding Hans's body had reignited my adrenaline and if I didn't do it now, the moment would be gone forever.

I had to pee in a cup.

The room was dark except for the wan light from the hallway. I yanked on the chain of the lamp but it didn't turn on. There was no time to waste checking the bulb. Using the flashlight from my cellphone, I illuminated the room's interior and searched for a receptacle. A jar of nuts sat on a shelf next to the desk. I unscrewed the top and dumped the nuts onto the desk and then went into the hallway in search of the bathroom.

Sometimes the wind blows you in very odd directions.

I rinsed out and dried the jar, and then, in the name of evidence, collected my sample and screwed the lid on tightly. It was then that I realized the nut jar would never fit in my vintage clutch handbag. Curses! I washed my hands (twice) and went back to the room, where I picked up a pair of jeans from the floor and wound it around the jar for camouflage. I pulled a plastic grocery store bag in the trash, and after shaking off some pistachio shells, I put the jean-and-pee bundle inside the bag and knotted the top. As soon as the police got here, I would make the handoff and be done with it.

Wilhelm remained in the room with me. With the sofa now unavailable, I sat in the chair behind the desk. My eyes were gradually adjusting to the darkness, and the piles of clothes that occupied nearly every surface of the room started to look less threatening and more like the condition in which I'd left my bedroom. I knew better than to tidy it up, but the mess added to my anxiety.

As I sat in the room, I heard a scratching sound. It came from somewhere to my left. I twisted and saw the blurry shape of a branch scraping the glass of the textured window behind me. The weather report had been for clear weather, but a clap of thunder would not have been unexpected.

My imagination went wild while I waited for the police to arrive. Lucy said the staff got off at nine. I'd woken up in the study at ten. Who had still been here?

For all the dangerous situations I'd found myself in, I'd never once knowingly been in the company of a killer, at least not for an extended stay. These people were all strangers, and any one of them could have done this. I glanced around the room while flashcards from Clue filtered through my mind. Rope. Candlestick. Wrench. Knife. Where was a lead pipe when you needed it?

My swirling thoughts were interrupted by sirens. Braeburn Castle sat back from the main road, so distant sirens weren't uncommon. But as the sirens grew in volume, I knew they were here in response to my call. The others, both innocent and guilty, would know *something* was up, but they wouldn't know what.

I heard the creak of the front door opening and a voice. "Hello? This is Detective Madden with the Ribbon Police." A pause. And then, "Samantha?"

Detective Madden and I had met a few years ago (my regular homicide detective was out of town on what was supposed to be a romantic getaway with his wife). (They'd divorced not long after, and I'd drawn a line through "Tahiti" as potential vacation spots.) Madden was a cross between Buddy Holly and a young Conan O'Brien: attractive and a little bit nerdy. After the second time I helped Madden with a case (my regular homicide detective had been about to retire and he'd gotten shot) (not fatally!), I learned Madden was interested in dating one of my friends. They'd gone out a few times, but I didn't know if it had petered out. This didn't seem like the time to ask him for a personal life update.

I went to the lobby. Madden was accompanied by two uniformed officers. I gave him a tight-lipped smile. "Tonight, you should call me Ms. Kidd," I said. I added, "the body is this way."

As I turned, I saw Lucy in the doorway to the bar. She had refilled her bourbon glass and raised it to her lips. Her eyes were glassy and her face was flushed more than it had been earlier. A gust of cool October wind had entered the castle with the police, and Lucy's blond hair lifted away from her face.

Madden turned to the officers and gave them instructions in a voice I couldn't overhear. I dubbed the scene in my mind: *find out how many people are here. Get names, statements, and contact information. Don't let anyone leave.*

I led Madden to the study and pointed at Hans's body on the sofa. Wilhelm sat on the desk, systematically licking his paw, and swiping it over his face. At least he was beyond suspicion.

"This is Hans," I said. "I don't know his last name."

"Braeburn," Lucy said from the doorway. The redness had left her skin, replaced by ghostly pale ivory. She was wrapped in a pashmina shawl, a shade of blue that complemented her eyes, though judging from how tightly she held it around her, it was warmth, not a need to accessorize, that had led her to use it. "His name was Hans Braeburn," she said softly.

"Braeburn? Like the castle?" Madden asked, raising his finger, and pointing toward the roof. She nodded.

"Hans was descended from the family that built this place?" I asked.

She shrugged like it was no big deal.

One of the uniformed officers stood in the doorway. Madden turned to him and said something I couldn't hear. The officer nodded and escorted Lucy out of the room. She looked back at Hans's body on the sofa. My earlier thought, *these people are all strangers* returned, followed with a caveat: *they're only strangers to me.*

Madden waited a long moment after Lucy and the officer left, and then turned back to me. "They're part of a secret society," I said. "There's five of them, well, there's more, but their meeting broke up early so they could interview me for potential membership. The interview panel was made up of five people." I held up my hand and ticked off names. "Lucy, Buck, Cecile, Ahn, and Hans."

Madden held up his index finger and flipped the cover back on a computer tablet. He made quick notes on the screen with his index finger, and then looked back up and gestured for me to continue.

"There was a glass of water set up for someone who never joined us." I bent down and picked up the plastic grocery store bag with my urine sample, feeling the flush of embarrassment. "This is going to sound strange…"

Madden nodded calmly as if hearing strange things happened every day. "Go on," he said.

"During my interview, I drank from the glass that had been set out for the person who didn't show. Almost immediately, I knew it wasn't plain water."

"How?"

"It tasted funny. And then my arms got heavy, and my legs couldn't support me. I had a hard time talking. I laid down on the carpet because I couldn't stand."

"Where was this?"

I pointed to the wall. "There's a clubroom at the end of the hallway. That's where the meeting and interview took place."

"What happened?"

"I woke up in here. On the sofa." I pointed to the sofa. Two EMTs had moved the piles of clothes off Hans so they could move his body to a gurney. "Lucy said she and Buck moved me, but I don't remember that."

"How long were you out?"

"I don't know. I got here at seven and they had me wait, and I woke up around ten. I was alone in here, and the room was dark. I found Lucy and Buck in the bar. They said Ahn went home and Hans and Cecile were still here, but I haven't seen anyone since."

Madden nodded along with me, occasionally saying "go on," or "interesting." When I finished talking, he said, "Sounds like the water was spiked."

"With what?" I asked.

"Hard to say. Any benzodiazepine would cause your body to shut down. Valium, Xanax, and Rohypnol. The drug affects the central nervous system and causes loss of muscle control." He checked his watch. "It's after midnight. Assuming you ingested the drug before eight, it would have been absorbed quickly and is in the process of being metabolized."

I raised the plastic bag. "You know how I said this might sound strange?" Madden nodded and looked warily at the bag. "After I called 911, I collected a urine sample."

He fought to contain his smile. "From anyone else, that would sound strange. But from you, it's par for the course."

5

NO SHAPE FOR THE FUN STUFF

TO HIS CREDIT, MADDEN DIDN'T ACT LIKE THE BAG HAD cooties. He looped the tied handles over his wrist and nodded his thank you. We stood in silence while the EMTs covered Hans with a thin blanket and then wheeled the gurney out of the room.

"Is there anything else you can tell me about Mr. Braeburn?" Madden asked once we were alone.

"I met him tonight. I think I was to be his replacement in the organization, but I don't think he was happy about it. Maybe he didn't want to leave."

"He was ninety-five," Madden said. "Probably legacy planning on the part of the club."

"I meant he was noticeably angry about it. I don't *think* it was personal…" My voice trailed off. "It couldn't have been. Aside from wearing brown tweed after eight, I did nothing to offend him."

"It *is* an odd choice for an evening soiree," Madden said.

"It's October, it's cool, and it's Bonnie Cashin," I said.

"The Fahrenheit Guild is a historical fashion society. I took a risk."

"Knowing what you do now, would you wear something different?"

"Sure. If I knew I was going to end up on the floor, I would have worn pants."

IT WAS after one by the time I arrived home. Despite my protests, Madden claimed there may still be traces of the drug in my system, which could affect my ability to drive. He insisted on having one of the officers give me a ride home and advised me to collect my recently purchased Refraction Blue Toyota GR Supra A91 tomorrow. I'd owned the limited edition car for less than a year, and I wasn't too happy about leaving it at the scene of a crime.

Nick had left the kitchen light on, and even though I spotted a pizza box on the counter, my stomach was still in knots over Hans's murder and I couldn't bring myself to eat. I glanced inside and then closed the lid and slid the box onto the bottom shelf in the fridge.

My mind was buzzing too much to sleep. I took a bubble bath. It had the desired response of relaxing me, so much so that Nick discovered me in tepid water a few hours later.

"Kidd," he said. "How long have you been in there?"

I opened my eyes and immediately felt cold. My arms were covered in gooseflesh, and my muscles twitched. Nick turned on the hot water, and after the initial luke-warm burst, heat warmed my feet. I curled forward and scooped hot water from the faucet onto my torso, and arms, and shoulders.

Nick was rumpled in the way people who travel tend to be when they finally return home and crash for twenty-four hours. Dark, curly hair equal parts matted and wild, eyes half-open, and sexy sleep voice. He scratched the side of his beard (it used to be between-shave stubble, but sometime in the past month, he'd done away with the shaving portion of his daily routine and now looked like the men on the cover of romcoms about hunters).

"I must have fallen asleep in here," I said.

I started to stand and he put his hand on my shoulder. "Stay," he said. "I'll throw some clothes in the dryer to warm them up." His eyes dropped from my face to my naked body. "Unless you'd rather warm up together…"

"Just get me to heat." I took his hand and with his help, got out of the water. He wrapped me in a large terrycloth towel then guided me to the bedroom. I was in no shape for the fun stuff. "Are chills a side effect of benzodi-azepines?" I asked.

"Roofies?" Nick asked. His expression went from concern to alarm. "What happened tonight?"

"Bed first," I said. I slid between the sheets. Nick turned on the electric blanket and set it on high, and then tucked the covers in around me. "Thank you."

The heat from the blanket created a warmth that slowly brought me back to a tolerable temperature. An orange glow came through the windows, hinting that it was close to sunrise. I was still tired and wanted to close my eyes.

"Do I need to call a doctor?" Nick asked.

"No," I said groggily. "Madden said the drug takes a few days to metabolize."

"Madden? Detective Madden? Why was he at your meeting?"

"I called him after I found the body," I said groggily.

"Kidd—"

I cut him off. "It's okay," I said. "He lived a long life." This time when I closed my eyes, Nick allowed me to sleep.

Hours later, I woke. It took me a moment to remember why I was under ten pounds of blankets, why I was asleep in broad daylight, and why there was a terrycloth robe bunched up around my waist. I dressed in a cashmere hoodie and matching jog pants and opened the door to the bedroom. Male voices floated up the stairs, and I tracked them to the kitchen where I found Nick and Detective Madden sitting across from each other.

"You're up," Nick said. He wrapped his arms around me. "Did we wake you?"

"No. I woke myself. What time is it?"

"Two thirty."

"In the afternoon?"

The two men smiled.

I filled a mug with fresh coffee and dropped into the chair at the end of the table. Nick sat down too. "I guess he told you what happened," I said to Nick, with a gesture toward Madden. It was nice not having to explain it myself. Madden was considerate that way.

"I gave him the highlights," Madden said. "We don't know much other than Mr. Braeburn died somewhere between eight and eleven o'clock last night. There were no visible wounds, and with what happened to you, we suspect poison. That's conjecture and doesn't leave this room. The coroner will tell us the cause of death after she conducts the autopsy."

"She?"

"Patti Detweiler. Appointed six months ago."

A female coroner, go figure. Girl Power had even infiltrated the death industry.

"Was she there last night?"

"She arrived after you left."

My dreams had been tortured, a likely combination of the drug and the murder. My brain had been searching for something new to link onto, a spark to shift me into a different direction where I could set aside the memory of Hans on the sofa. Before I recognized it, my mind shifted toward what it would be like to be the coroner for Berks County. What were the qualifications? Did you need friends in high places? Was there a test?"

"No," Nick said.

"What?"

"I know how your mind works."

He did, and he was probably right.

"Can you tell us anything else?" I asked Detective Madden.

"Hans Braeburn was the oldest living member of the Braeburn family. He moved to the states after World War II and was the lone family member to survive a fire not long after."

"He didn't live there, did he? In the castle?"

"Yes," Madden said. "He kept it private. He probably cared more about his solitude and routine than the income he could have made renting it out. From what I know, the only time it's open is for your club meetings."

"I think it's safe to say it's not my club."

Nick put his hand over mine. "What exactly happened to you last night?"

I looked at Madden. "I thought you told him."

"The details are yours to tell. I came here to check on you and see if you wanted a ride to the castle to claim your car."

"Oh. Yes. That would be great."

Madden excused himself and went to the restroom while I recounted the previous evening to Nick. Confrontation with Hans/drank the tainted water/woke up in the study/talked to two members of the guild in the bar/found Hans's body. Even using the shorthand married people develop, I was mid-account when Madden returned.

"Did I hear you say you talked to two members of the guild in the bar?" he asked. "Which two?"

"Lucy and Buck." I squeezed my eyes shut and retrieved their full names. "Lucy Francis and Buckley Owen Hollinger. The fourth." I opened my eyes. "They were helping themselves to bourbon. I didn't learn much about either one of them except that Buck has a trust fund that seems to be the only thing he likes about his family."

"And Lucy? Did she say anything about her family?"

"No," I said. "Why? Is she rich too?"

Madden studied my face. "She didn't tell you?"

"Tell me what?"

"Lucy was Hans's granddaughter."

6

A POLICE MATTER

"That means Lucy stands to benefit from Hans's death," I said.

"It also means Lucy lost her grandfather," Nick reminded me.

"Yes," I said, staring at his face. "I suppose it does."

I remembered Lucy's coloring, flushed and red at the bar and then ghostly pale when the police arrived. She'd made a point of bringing up Buck's family but hadn't mentioned hers. It was possible she thought I already knew, and equally possible she'd wanted it to remain a secret.

I finished my coffee and left with Madden. Nick would have given me a ride, but I'd relied heavily on him before choosing my car, and these days, I preferred to keep favors in the "will you make me dinner?" category.

Madden was a thoughtful man, not prone to idle chitchat or forced conversation. Braeburn Castle was about five miles from my house, and I assumed we'd drive in silence. I assumed wrong.

"I had an ulterior motive for coming to your house today," Madden said when we were about half a mile into the drive. "I wanted to talk to you alone. This case is going to occupy most of my time, but there's an unrelated situation that requires your help."

I perked up. "A police matter?"

"It may be." The light in front of us changed, and instead of accelerating through the yellow, Madden slowed the car far in advance. "Cat's nephew is missing. The Philadelphia police are looking for him, but so far, no leads. He's fourteen years old, so he doesn't have a car, but he could have hitchhiked out of town or possibly—" the light changed and Madden turned right. "—temporarily borrowed a vehicle."

"You said he's fourteen."

"Cat says he knows how to drive."

"Is her car missing?"

"No, and his dad drives a motorcycle."

"I know," I said absentmindedly.

It had been a long time since I thought about Cat's brother. Not since I'd gotten married. Because Cat's brother, Dante, was the type of guy who could temporarily distract you from things like long-term commitments.

Dante was, at first glance, a rough-and-ready tough guy who might motivate people to cross the street before passing. His jet black hair and long sideburns were reminiscent of the rockabilly movement, and the rest of his outfit: white T-shirt, worn-in jeans, black leather jacket, and motorcycle boots, were straight out of the how-to-dress-like-Joey-Ramone playbook. He'd entered my life with a bang, provided an exciting counterpoint to Nick's dependability, and inspired me to question a lot of what I thought I knew about myself. He taught me most of what I knew about investigating a crime scene and a little of what I knew about kissing. I suppose Nick owed him a thank you.

I'd acquired the intel that Dante had a son by accident, or more accurately, by snooping. There was a photo of the three of them: mom, dad, son, in a drawer in Dante's kitchen, and I'd been staying at his place while avoiding some trouble. As soon as I saw it, I knew it was none of my business. But when Dante found out, he volunteered the truth. The pregnancy had been unplanned, and while the relationship hadn't worked out, the idea of having a child appealed to the soon-to-be mother. Dante agreed to do what was best for her and the child, and within a year, there was a baby boy.

Who, according to Madden, was now missing.

"His name is Jameson, right?" I asked. Madden nodded. "If I remember correctly, he lives with his mother in Philadelphia, and Cat's brother sees him on occasion."

"New Jersey," Madden corrected. "They moved."

"But you said the Philadelphia police had been notified."

"He was visiting for the summer. His mother thought he would benefit from being around his father. Fourteen is a pivotal age for a boy."

I thought back to my fourteen-year-old days. What was that, eighth grade? Was there anything significant about that year? The memory felt bland, like filler inserted into a life that had not known real excitement until almost a decade later when I moved to New York.

Ribbon, Pennsylvania hadn't been nearly this exciting when I was a kid.

We arrived at Braeburn Castle, and Madden parked next to my bright blue sports car. He didn't turn off the engine.

"Have you met him?" I asked.

"Once," Madden said. "Christmas. He struck me as a bright kid who needed a male role model."

"Translation: he's a teenage boy rebelling against his mother's attempts at discipline."

"Something like that." Madden smiled. "Cat has her hands full with her baby, but I can tell she's worried." He grew quiet, but it felt like he wasn't done.

"There's something else, isn't there?" I asked.

He nodded. "There's been a string of crimes in Philadelphia. The victims aren't that much older than Jameson. What little I know about him missing fits the pattern. I can't tell you anything more, but Cat's right to worry."

It seemed foolish to confirm that Madden and Cat were still dating. He admitted to having spent a major holiday with her family, and his concern for her was evident.

I thanked him for confiding in me and we went our separate ways. I would have liked to follow him into the castle and see it in the daytime, less scary than the night before, but Madden was by-the-book, and his book probably didn't have a chapter on giving tours of crime scenes to well-dressed amateur sleuths. I backed out of my space and drove half a mile away and then pulled over to the shoulder of the road. There was a phone call I needed to make, but it wasn't one I wanted to make from home.

I knew I should call Cat, but before that, I needed to check on Dante.

He answered on the third ring. "Yo," he said.

"It's Samantha."

"I recognized the number."

"I'm not programmed into your phone?"

"You were. I deleted you after meeting an attractive bartender. Things looked promising for a while. Seemed better not to have a questionable number of women in my contacts."

"So, it wasn't personal," I said.

"With you, it's always personal."

There was something about Dante that immediately brought out the flirt in me. I never once questioned if I'd made the right decision by marrying Nick, but two years into our marriage, the honeymoon heat had started to normalize. Stresses from Nick's sneaker business kept him on edge, and his travel schedule kept us apart, and there was my pesky habit of occasionally rubbing elbows with the criminal kind that sometimes interfered with romance. We still enjoyed our time together in bed but more and more often that time was spent eating pretzels and ice cream while watching a movie.

Dante's and my time together usually involved that criminal element I'd mentioned, which may have contributed to a heightened sense of danger and thus excitement. The last time I saw him had been at a Christmas party at my house. It was after the murder of Cat's cheating husband had been solved, and the evening had a celebratory vibe. Dante learned that I'd said yes to Nick's proposal, and that was that.

So much had transpired since then, it felt like a lifetime ago.

"I heard about Jameson," I said.

"From?"

"Madden."

"He called you?"

"We ran into each other recently." I didn't want to bring up Hans or the Fahrenheit Guild, not while Dante was dealing with his missing son. I stretched the truth a bit. "It was an industry event. The last place I would have imagined seeing him."

"Right," Dante said. The response was abstract, unimportant in the grand scheme of things. It was a verbal marker to indicate he'd heard me talking but didn't care all that much about what I'd said. I supposed he had more pressing things on his mind.

"What are you doing to find him?"

"Knocking on doors, putting out feelers, contacting his friends. He got into a fight in the neighborhood and his mom asked me if I'd take him in for the month. She thought I'd be a good influence."

It was like what Madden had said. "He must have loved spending time with you. He's old enough to see you differently. Like man to man, not boy to man."

"I don't think that's how he felt," Dante said slowly. "But I wouldn't know."

"How come? Did he say or do something when he arrived?"

"That's it. His mom said she dropped him off at the house, but Cat said he never showed up."

7

FOR OLD TIME'S SAKE

THAT DIDN'T FIT WITH WHAT DETECTIVE MADDEN HAD told me, and these seemed like important facts to get straight. "Hold up," I said. "Did you say he never made it to your house?"

"Right."

"So technically you don't know how long he's been missing."

"Linda said she dropped him off out front and waited until he let himself in. I was out getting groceries. When I got home, Cat said he hadn't arrived yet. I didn't call Linda until a few hours later, and that's when we put our two stories together."

It took a moment to remember Linda was Dante's ex, but after that fact dropped into place, I caught up quickly. Dante and Linda had established a friendly relationship for Jameson's benefit, but other than that, I didn't know anything about her.

This account—what Linda told Dante about the day Jameson went missing—felt full of holes. It was the Swiss cheese of information that made Linda look good, but what if that wasn't what happened? What if after she and Jameson had fought, he left for Dante's on his own but never made it there? What if he took off for a less family-oriented adventure, or worse, what if something bad had happened? It was Philadelphia, after all. Bad things happened there all the time.

"Since the last time you saw me, I've been working on my habit of offering unsolicited help," I said. "But for old time's sake, is there anything I can do?"

"Maybe," Dante said. "Can you check my apartment in Ribbon? Jameson knows I have a place there, and if he found the address, he might have thought it would make a good hideout."

"Sure," I said without hesitation. It was the least I could do.

"I can have a locksmith meet you if you don't still have my key."

"I still have it," I said quickly.

"Good," Dante said. "Makes things easy."

The conversation had taken us to new territory. Even when we'd worked together to solve the murder of Cat's husband, Dante had leaned into his role as mentor-slash-spirit guide. The ease with which he walked away said I'd been a distraction, someone to entertain him while he was here in my hometown, or maybe that was something I'd told myself to feel better about moving on first.

It was after four. I drove to Dante's place, an apartment that was, coincidentally, less than two miles from Braeburn Castle. The apartment was built on the side of a hill. Thirty-nine steps led up to his front door (I'd counted them once).

I parked on the street and approached the entrance. After last night, I welcomed the diversion. I accumulated over a dozen unclaimed newspapers left scattered across the path and unlocked the front door.

The interior was neat. If anyone were living here uninvited, they took great pains to leave things the way they'd found them. I dropped the newspapers onto the coffee table and ran my finger over the table's surface, leaving a trail in the dust. No one had been here in a long time.

To be certain, I checked the trash cans (empty) and the electricity (on). I looked out the back door, but aside from leaves that had fallen from nearby trees, there was nothing to see. I opened a couple of windows and allowed a cool autumn breeze to pass through the interior, and I checked the cabinets for a snack. A bag of multigrain Splits pretzels sat on a shelf between a stockpile of Campbell's soup. The pretzels were about to expire. It was my duty to make sure they didn't go to waste.

I opened the bag and carried it to the futon, then, recognizing how neat the place was, returned to the kitchen and put the pretzels on a paper towel to avoid crumbs. Dante's apartment was a studio, so what you saw was what you got. I returned to the futon. After eating enough pretzels to silence the rumble in my tummy, I closed the bag and returned it to the pantry. Until I heard Jameson had been found, I knew stopping in here would become a daily thing.

My phone rattled in my handbag. I dug it out and saw "Carl" on the screen. Carl Collins was a crime reporter for the *Ribbon Eagle*. Despite sharing an employer, our paths at the paper only crossed when I stepped into his lane.

"Hi, Carl," I answered wearily. "What do you want to know?"

"Nice company you're keeping these days. Really traded down in the world, haven't you, Kidd?"

The cell connection wasn't great. I got up from the futon and wandered across the room, hoping to pick up a stronger signal. Carl's voice skipped in and out until I stood in front of Dante's bookcase, where the reception appeared to be as good as it was going to get. "What are you talking about?"

"The Fahrenheit Guild? Braeburn Castle? Nazis? Stop me when this gets familiar."

I felt the room grow cold and repeated back to him the word that didn't make sense. "Nazis?"

"The founder of the club was a Nazi. Moved here before World War II ended. Probably why they met in secret. There's a hush-hushed history of German companies working for the Nazis back in the day. I bet fashion is no different. Monty said we should work together on a piece."

Monty was our editor at the paper, and the only time Monty told Carl and me to collaborate was when he thought it would sell more papers. More likely, Carl wanted to exploit me for his story.

"This is a joke, right? Look. I know we have a deal. I'm sorry I didn't call you right away, but it was the middle of the night, and some stuff happened earlier that left me a little foggy. There's no way the murder made the morning paper. I'll tell you the same thing I told the police."

"You were there," he said slowly, not an accusation, but a realization. It was as if he was putting it all together. "You were at the castle when Hans Braeburn's body was found, weren't you? I don't believe this. You are the single luckiest person I know."

"Your definition of luck is questionable."

"If you were a crime reporter, you'd be dangerous competition."

"Then I guess *you're* lucky I'm not. Do you want to hear about last night or not?"

"Buy you dinner?"

"Deal."

We agreed on a time and place, and I disconnected. Between the two of us, Carl wasn't the only one who needed information. I stayed in the good cell reception spot and called Nick. "You should eat the leftover pizza for dinner," I said. "I talked to Carl, and we're going to meet so I can tell him about last night."

"Where are you?" he asked.

I went with vague. "Close to downtown. We're meeting at Pappa's Pizza."

"Kidd, I don't want to sound like a nagging husband, but when do you plan to clean up your clothes? It looks like someone detonated a clothing bomb in the house."

"I forgot about them."

"I moved everything into the spare bedroom, but with the racks of sneaker samples, it's getting hard to move around in there." He paused for a moment and then added, "I don't think I fully realized how many clothes you have."

"I'll take care of it," I said. "Tonight." Nick didn't say anything. "I will. I promise. After I finish with Carl, I'll come home and box everything up. Once my clothes are back in the attic, the spare bedroom is all yours."

"You don't have to get it done tonight, but soon would

be a big help. I can work out of the basement, but I can't store inventory down there. One rainstorm and all of my stock would be ruined."

I'd been standing in a spot in front of Dante's bookshelves, and while Nick talked, I ran my finger across the spines. Dante's reading tastes weren't surprising: Jack Reacher, Howard Stern, Andy Weir. But tucked between books about bros was a small turquoise hardcover. I tilted my head and read the title, and then smiled. The discovery was equal parts charming and fortuitous, considering my conversation with Nick. I put my finger on the top of the book and tipped it toward me. *The Life-Changing Magic of Tidying Up.*

"Tonight," I said again. "I'll be a folding machine. Productivity like you've never seen."

Nick chuckled. "Have fun with Carl," he said. "And enjoy your pizza."

We hung up and I removed the book from the shelf. Maybe I wasn't done learning from Dante after all.

8

VEGETABLES

CARL WAS WAITING FOR ME IN A BOOTH AT PAPPA'S PIZZA. He'd traded his trademark blue seersucker suit for a navy blue one over a white shirt and blue knit tie. His entire look had been modeled on *Kolchak: The Night Stalker,* though Carl's cultivated version of dogged reporter lacked the flirtatious charm of Darren McGavin's performance. I'd recently encouraged Carl to collaborate with another reporter, a la *All the President's Men,* and he'd had the nerve to say life wasn't like a movie.

If Carl's life was *Kolchak: The Night Stalker,* then mine was *Murder She Wrote.* Ribbon, the town where I'd grown up complaining that nothing ever happened, had become my Cabot Cove. The people in my life chose not to make inappropriate jokes about it, and the people outside of my life read about me in the paper. It kept my circle of friends both intimate and trustworthy. Carl was somewhere in that range, but not quite. No matter what happened, he'd always want something from me.

I slid into the booth. "I was thinking large, upside-down pizza. Does that work for you?"

"Order whatever you want. I'm not eating."

"You asked me here for dinner."

"You want dinner. I want information. It's a fair trade."

"If I order a large pizza and you don't eat, people are going to think I'm a glutton."

"Since when do you care what other people think?"

He had a point. "Wait here."

I went to the counter and placed my order. The construction was what made an upside-down special: squares of mozzarella cheese were placed on the dough, and then the sauce was added on top. In the oven, the sauce formed into a crust. The dough was thicker than you found on Neapolitan pizzas. It was a nice change of pace for people like me who had pizza three times a week. (Sometimes four.)

I grabbed two bottles of Birch Beer from the refrigerated case and carried them to the table. Carl twisted the cap off his and rested it next to his phone. "Can I record you?" he asked.

I shrugged my consent.

"I need a verbal yes or no."

"Is it already on?"

"Yeah."

"Geez," I said. "This is Samantha Kidd. I give my consent to allow Carl Collins to record this conversation."

"Okay. Tell me about last night."

I recounted the events from the Fahrenheit Guild interview. Carl had his methods for learning of crimes around Ribbon, but he didn't know the details. This was the third time I'd relayed the story, and somewhere along

the way, it had become less memory and more memo-
rization.

"What do you know about the Fahrenheit Guild?" I
asked him. "Have you heard of them before?"

He held up his finger and waggled it back and forth.
"No questions. *I'm* interviewing *you.*"

"Do you give your consent to record this interview?"

"No." He pressed pause. "I've heard about them in
passing. Ribbon has a lot of secret clubs. Scratch the
surface of this town and you'd be amazed at what you
find."

"You mentioned Nazis."

"Hans Braeburn was one. He came to the states in
1944 and helped run a Hitler Youth camp in Buyersville
into the Fifties."

I felt the shock that comes with learning that something unsavory had existed in a town about an hour from
where you live. "But the war was over by then. Germany
lost."

Carl tipped his head from side to side. "Yes, and no.
The war ended, but a lot of people thought if they indoc-
trinated kids, they would grow up and resume the battle."

"How public is the knowledge that Hans was a Nazi?"

"It wasn't the first layer of the onion."

Reporters, I'd learned, liked to talk about vegetables.
Layers of onion were research. Cabbage was day-old
news. I'd tried to make artichoke an expression once, but
it hadn't stuck. I still didn't know why.

Carl was an effective reporter. He had access to the
city paper's archives and grew up with an old-school
respect for colorful details and deep research. Most of
what he needed could be found online, but he was a

frequent visitor to the city's hardcopy archives and spent considerable time in the basement flipping through back issues. It served the purpose of giving him context to those details, sometimes seeing an old news story sandwiched between an ad for a now-defunct department store or a story about wartime rationing.

The pizza arrived, and Carl's phone went into sleep mode while I ate. He said nothing when I eased two slices onto my plate, but he shook his head when I reached for the third.

"Don't judge me. I've seen inside your car. When's the last time you had a meal that didn't come from McDonald's?"

"Point taken," he said.

"Besides, I haven't eaten in twenty-four hours," I said.

"Didn't you turn forty this year? Your metabolism is going to screech to a halt and you're not going to be able to fit into any of your clothes."

"Pizza and I have an understanding," I said. "This is practically health food."

I called it quits after the third slice, not because I didn't want a fourth, but because I didn't want Carl's commentary.

I gestured to a man at the front for a box and then turned back to Carl. "How'd you know I was interviewing for a spot in the Fahrenheit Guild?" I asked idly.

"I have a source."

I narrowed my eyes. Carl's source had to come from either the castle or the police. It was one thing for him to learn of a murder from listening to the police scanner, but another for someone to have called him directly. "I got home after one. The police were still there and showed no signs of leaving. The paperboys start delivering at five. When did this report come in?"

"You're not in any danger," he said. "Hans Braeburn was old. He was diagnosed with colorectal cancer, for which there's no cure. His dad built the castle, and he moved in when he was eighteen. His parents died shortly after he married and he inherited it all and then quietly inserted himself into our town."

"Where's his wife?"

"She died in the same fire that killed his parents. Wine cellar. Hans never remarried. If you weren't plugged into his politics and you met him casually, you'd probably think he was a nice, old, Pennsylvania Dutch man, but Hans Braeburn was not what he seemed."

"Do you think that's why someone killed him? They found out who he was or what he'd done?"

"It's possible."

"But if he was murdered as revenge, why wait until he's ninety-five to do it? He wasn't the picture of health, and he didn't exactly exude happiness."

"That brings up the question of motive," Carl said. "You said Lucy Francis was one of the members. Maybe she got tired of waiting for her inheritance."

"She went out of her way to keep her relation to Hans a secret. How'd you find out?"

"It's called research. You should try it."

"You had to know that there was something to research first," I said.

He shrugged. "You know the drill on murder stories. You focus on the victim. I searched on Hans Braeburn and found the story about the fire that killed his parents and wife. Turns out Hans hadn't been a faithful husband, and a woman came forward and claimed her daughter was his."

"Lucy?"

"Lucy's mother.

I'd been so focused on the story of Hans that I hadn't pieced together what this new information meant about Lucy. "Do you think she knew?" I leaned forward and lowered my voice. "She had to know. It's her family history. She doesn't look like she's hurting for money, but—"

"But the people who are hurting for money go to great lengths to make it look like they're not," he finished. He checked his watch. "I've got another meeting tonight. You mind if I leave?"

"Not as long as you pay first," I said. I grinned and Carl grinned back. Our editor would hate knowing Carl's expense account was being used to treat me, another employee, to dinner, but picking up the tab during a source interview was standard operating procedure amongst reporters.

"Done," he said. He carried the receipt to the register while I closed the box.

There was one thing nagging at me about Hans's murder, and that was the way his body had been staged. If Hans had been found reclining on the sofa, or in a chair, or any other expected place for a ninety-five-year-old body to rest for a moment, I doubted any of us would have found it suspicious. The night had already been charged with tension after my collapse, and a heart attack wouldn't have been outside the realm of possibility.

But Hans been buried under stacks of clothes. Jeans, from what I remembered. The study had been filled with piles and piles of denim, most folded, some not. Someone had decided to use the study for storage. And what had Hans said when he first introduced me? He was going to rethink my nomination as his successor.

That meant he'd chosen me. Why? I'd never heard of him before, didn't have a connection to him, or to the guild. I was a name in the paper.

There was another troubling detail that probably meant nothing. During my interview, Hans had asked me about jeans. I'd assumed it was a test, especially after being criticized for my Bonnie Cashin ensemble, but maybe not. The truth was, I didn't know enough about the dynamics of the group to know much more than what I'd seen. I didn't even know the cause of death.

I slid out of the booth, propped the pizza box next to my hip, and caught up with Carl.

"Did you remember something?" he asked. He pulled out his phone. I waved it away.

"How did Hans die?" I asked.

"The police said the coroner would determine the cause of death, but I heard he was buried under a pile of jeans."

"He was. You think he was suffocated?"

"It's a working theory. Should be easy to prove. All they need is to find a pair with a death mask."

9

IT DIDN'T FEEL RANDOM

THE THREE (AND A HALF) SLICES OF PIZZA IN MY STOMACH somersaulted at the thought that someone had suffocated Hans with a pair of jeans. I'd thought he'd been murdered and buried underneath the pile, but what if he'd been given the same poison as I had and hadn't been able to fight back? What if he'd been aware of what was happening to him as it took place?

"I'm headed to the coroner now," Carl said. "You want to join me?" He pointed to his Mustang.

As excited as I was by the prospect of meeting the girl coroner, I had other plans. "No, you go. I've got some other things to deal with."

"Sure," he said. He got into his car and rolled down the window. "Thanks for the story, Sam. If you need anything, give me a call."

I sat inside my car with the air conditioning on high for a few minutes after Carl drove away. I'd heard of Nazi soldiers coming to the states, keeping their war crimes to themselves, but Hans had moved to the states when he was eighteen. He lived in a little Pennsylvania town for seventy-seven years and now he was dead.

It didn't feel random.

When I finally felt better, I secured the pizza box on the back seat, buckled up, and started the engine. The car purred like a cat. I left Pappa's parking lot, waited at the light by the corner, and then pulled out onto State Hill Road. About a mile into my drive home, I slowed for another light and a car pulled up next to me. I knew what was coming, so I lowered my window.

My previous car had been a hand-me-down from my mom, and when it was no longer operable (thanks to the local mafia), I'd taken my good old time choosing this one. It was sexy and unique, not exactly good for covert operations, but excellent for meeting random men at intersections. More often than I would have imagined, cars driven by men pulled up alongside me at intersections and the drivers asked questions about the Supra's performance. After three times, I memorized the spec sheet so I sounded more informed.

"Nice ride," the man in the lane next to me said. "How many horses?"

"Three hundred eighty-two."

"Torque?"

"Three sixty-eight."

He nodded his approval. "Sweet." The light changed and he inched forward. I put my foot on the gas and left him in my dust.

Ever since I'd chosen the limited edition sportscar, I'd gained access to a club I hadn't known existed. I'd first recommended it to someone else, but when it was still available a week later, I decided the person I really wanted it for was me.

I drove home. Nick's truck wasn't there. I put the left-over pizza in the kitchen and carried Dante's book to the spare bedroom. Nick hadn't exaggerated. The room was a mess: every surface was covered with linen, silk, and cotton. Logan, my black cat, sat amidst a pile of cashmere that Nick had placed on top of the desk. Logan stared at me as if to say, "You did it, not me."

I went back downstairs and called Dante. "Yo," he answered.

"It's Samantha," I said. "Have you heard anything?"

"A couple of businesses remember seeing Jameson in the area, but that's it. Anything there?"

"Your apartment looks like it's been empty for a while. Newspapers on the yard, dust on the surfaces inside. I don't think he's crashing there."

Dante was silent. I wanted to offer good news, hope of some kind, but I didn't know enough about the situation to be of help. I saw the book on the counter. "I borrowed a book from your library. I hope you don't mind."

"Take whatever you want," he said absentmindedly. It wasn't said out of generosity. Dante's mind was far away from his personal belongings. Bringing up the book had been stupid.

"Keep me posted, okay? If you hear anything." I didn't like how that sounded. *If.* "or, when Jameson comes home, have Cat give me a call."

"Sure. Thanks." He disconnected.

I didn't know this Dante well. He'd always been calm, almost humorously distanced from the dangerous situations we'd occasionally found ourselves drawn to, and he'd shown me compassion at a time when I felt isolated. Once he'd opined that we were a lot alike, and I'd disagreed. But wasn't my ability to focus on a borrowed book instead of his missing son the same as his inappropriate flirtations while we were dealing with a murderer?

I didn't like what that said about me, and despite all my growth in the category of offering unsolicited help, I couldn't sit by and do nothing. I called Carl.

"Have you heard anything about a string of crimes involving young men in Philadelphia?" I asked.

"Does this have to do with Hans Braeburn?"

"No. Different matter." I stopped myself short of telling Carl about Dante's missing son. Carl was a reporter, and a story was a story. I didn't want to do anything that might make matters worse for Dante.

"Depending on the nature of the crimes, it might not be a big story. Plus, Philadelphia news would be in the *Post*. You could call them."

I chewed my lip and stared at Dante's book on the counter. I'd collected about a dozen newspapers from Dante's yard and left them on the dining room table. If they'd been reporting on the story, chances were I could find everything I needed to know without alerting anyone else.

I made up an excuse to get off the phone with Carl. There was nothing left to do but tackle the mess in the spare bedroom. The good thing about spending the day in a hoodie and jog pants was that, unlike days when I dressed to the nines, I didn't need to change. I left my shoes by the door and picked up a pile of clothes, kicking at garments still on the floor to make space for organization.

Let's see. I've organized my clothes by type, color, season, and decade. How should I do it now? What would be the optimal way to repack everything so the next time it won't result in the destructive scene of fabric warfare?

Technically, this was tidying up, so I consulted Dante's book. Maybe Marie Kondo had some insider tips for me, something more useful than tucking socks inside shoes when you pack. I bet she had *wicked* storage solutions.

I returned to the spare bedroom, shifted a pile of clothes from the chair behind Logan, and settled in to read. Research in the name of productivity, I told myself. Consult the experts. Reading this book was going to be a time-saver.

TWO HOURS LATER, Nick found me buried knee-deep in piles. There was no path between me and the door, which made a hello kiss near-impossible. "Making progress?" he asked dubiously.

"Oh my gosh! The problem isn't that I need more space for storage, the problem is that I can't tell if my clothes spark joy." I held up a ribbed tank top that said "Fierce." "Does this spark joy?" I pulled the garment to my chest. "Am I not doing it right?"

"Doing what right?"

"Testing my clothes for joy-sparking. Marie says I'm supposed to put everything I own on the floor and then pick each item up and hold it to see if it sparks joy. This is everything I own, but the process is a little overwhelming." I took a few quick, shallow breaths. I was possibly hyperventilating.

"You don't mean…" Nick's voice trailed off. He glanced around the room and then walked away. I would have tried to follow him, but a barrier of vintage tracksuits blocked the path. A few seconds later, he returned. "Your side of the closet is empty."

"I know. Marie said to gather up everything I own, so I did."

"Who is this Marie?"

"Marie Kondo. The tidying-up expert." Dante's book was under one of the non-joy-sparking piles, but to be safe, I didn't dig it out.

"What about the coat closet?"

"Got it.

"Basement?"

"Got it."

"Dryer?"

"There are clothes in the dryer?" I dropped the Fierce T-shirt and pulled my foot straight up, then looked for the best place to step. To keep my balance, I held my arms out on either side. I felt like the Karate Kid.

"You don't have to do this," Nick said. "You're a fashion person. You're expected to have a lot of clothes."

"Yes, but do I wear them? All of them? What am I keeping them for? I gained ten pounds since we got married and I can't even fit in half of them!"

"I like those ten pounds," Nick said.

As sweet as that was, I didn't let it derail me. I snagged a slinky, spaghetti-strapped slip dress from the mid-nineties. "Ten pounds would make all the difference in a dress like this." The idea of wearing a revealing slip dress did not spark joy. I tossed it onto a section of the carpet that housed two pairs of corduroy OP shorts and a pink satin bomber jacket that had "Pink Ladies" embroidered on the back.

Nick stifled a smile. "Is that your giveaway pile?"

"Yes. Why?"

He stepped around two piles and bent down, looping his finger through one of the spaghetti straps of the discarded dress. "I don't think you want to get rid of this one. To be sure, maybe you should model it for me later. There might be some joy sparking still left in it." He flashed me a devilish smile, and I snatched the dress from his hand.

"You're no help," I said. "But while you're standing there, can you hand me that pink satin jacket? I don't want to make any rash decisions."

10

VENGEANCE?

Nick left to retrieve the clothes from the dryer. I dug Dante's book out from under a pile of non-joy-sparking clothes and checked to see if he'd written his name inside. I hadn't told Nick about hearing from Dante, and while the wedding ring on my finger and the regular sleeping arrangements spoke to my commitment, there was underlying jealousy of Dante that Nick hadn't quite shaken. I didn't need my latest project to be the catalyst for marital discord.

When Nick returned with the laundry basket, I'd added a cropped chartreuse sweatshirt and two pairs of torn and faded jeans that used to belong to my dad to the discard pile. Nick set the basket by the door. "Where do you want these?"

"Anywhere there's room," I said. "I think I need a break."

He kicked a space on the floor for the basket, then held out his hand and guided me through the mess. We went downstairs to the kitchen and I dropped into a dining room chair.

My shoulder muscles ached. I wrapped my right arm around my torso and massaged my left shoulder. Sorting clothes was hard physical labor.

Nick came up behind me and used both hands to knead my shoulder muscles. I felt the tension slowly eke out of me. I closed my eyes and relaxed. "What do you know about Nazis living in Ribbon?" I asked. Nick's fingers stopped moving. "Please don't stop," I said.

He started kneading again. "Nothing," he said. "why?"

"Carl Collins told me Hans Braeburn was a Nazi."

"Carl wouldn't say that unless he had facts to back it up."

"I know. He's working on a story about Hans's murder. He said that part wasn't the first layer of the onion."

"Then this story is going to be more of an exposé."

I twisted around in my chair and looked up at Nick. "Would that be a reason for someone to commit murder? If Hans had kept it a secret and someone found out? Or if they've known that Hans has been living here all this time? Could a need for vengeance become so strong that someone acted on a repressed impulse after three quarters of a century?"

"Is that how long he's lived in Ribbon?" he asked.

"Seventy-seven years."

"It's possible," he said. "That's a polarizing subject."

"I don't get it, though. Hans was ninety-five. Why not wait him out?"

"It's possible the killer already waited seventy-seven years."

"You're suggesting the killer was Hans's age."

Nick shook his head. "I'm not suggesting anything. But if someone was waiting for karmic justice, seventy-seven years is a long time. If the killer wasn't in good health, he or she might have felt like they were running out of time to act." He bent down and kissed the top of my head. "Seems like a clear motive," he added.

The next morning, stiff from tidying up until two in the morning, I dressed in a vintage pair of white bootcut Levi's, a blue and white striped cotton shirt knotted at the waist, and a faded and frayed denim jean jacket. I stepped into camel leather boots with chunky heels and slung a vintage leather mail carrier bag across my chest for use as my handbag. I'd come across every piece somewhere after midnight, and the joy of finding clothes I'd completely forgotten I owned overrode the panic over needing better storage. I tied my hair into a loose ponytail and put on gold-rimmed aviator shades that matched my gold earrings.

Nick was on a call with China. This had become a necessary evil since he started designing sneakers, but we both hoped a stateside solution would eliminate the strain of constant travel plus the twelve-hour time difference with his factory manager. I waved goodbye and left.

I drove to Dante's apartment. A white Ford Explorer pulled up next to me at a traffic light, and a man in his sixties leaned out his window. "Nice ride," he said. "What kind of mirror cups are those?"

"Carbon fiber," I said.

"Those wheels an upgrade?"

"Nope. Matte black alloy comes standard."

He nodded. "I saw a guy driving around in a car like that last week."

"Must have been my husband," I said with a tight smile. "He likes to borrow it."

The man grinned his approval. The light changed, and I left him in my dust.

I parked in front of Dante's apartment, retrieved today's paper, and went inside. The place looked as it had yesterday. A thin trail was visible on the coffee table from where I'd dragged my finger through the dust. Sometime during the night, the Howard Stern biography had tipped into the space left behind from *The Life-Changing Magic of Tidying Up,* making the vacant spot less visible.

After checking outside the back door, I helped myself to a pile of multigrain Splits and pulled each old *Philadelphia Post* newspaper out of its plastic bag, then arranged them in order of date with the most recent on top. There were fourteen, more than I'd originally counted. I started reading and found what I was looking for in the third one.

It was a story about a sixteen-year-old boy who'd woken up in his underwear in a public park. He claimed not to know how he got there or what had happened. His parents, once notified, would not submit to any physical tests, and took him home.

The second account, similar in nature, came two days later. Seventeen-year-old boy picked up on charges of indecent exposure. He spent the night in a local holding cell and was released to his parents the next morning. They had no comment.

After flipping through the rest of the papers, I had a list of five different crimes, all involving teen boys, all involving various degrees of undress. The third and fourth had submitted to DNA testing, and no evidence of sexual molestation was present. The fifth one was the oldest at nineteen. He'd been arrested for shoplifting. The store pressed charges, and he'd gone to jail. Two days after being released on bail, he went missing.

Every article included a picture of the boy in question. They looked like teenaged boys should look: skinny, a little rough, and full of attitude. But the last picture was the one that stopped me in my tracks. The picture showed two boys, and the one in the background was familiar.

Aside from the photo I'd found in Dante's kitchen drawer, I'd never seen Jameson, but I recognized him immediately. The problem was that I recognized him from somewhere else. The caption identified him as the victim's friend, Jameson Lestes, but the boy in the photo was the redhead I'd seen at Braeburn Castle.

11

COMMONLY KNOWN AS A DILEMMA

I WAS AS SURE OF IT AS I COULD BE, CONSIDERING THE photo was a grainy newspaper reproduction, and the guy I'd seen had facial scruff hiding half his face. I struggled to make the two pieces of information fit but realized I was wasting time. I called Detective Madden.

I identified myself when he answered. "When you questioned the staff at Braeburn Castle, did you talk to anyone unusual? Maybe some young, part-time help?"

There was the sound of rustling, and then, "No. I talked to Marguerite and her husband. Why?"

This was commonly known as a dilemma. Madden was a by-the-book cop who was tasked with solving Hans Braeburn's homicide, and he trusted procedure and left no room for mistakes. But the redhead, if I was correct, was Dante's son. And Dante's sister was dating Detective Madden.

The dilemma should have been Madden's, but until I told him what I knew, there was no way to predict which direction he'd turn.

"There was someone else," I said cautiously. "He might have left by the time you arrived. I got the impression he helped around the castle. I saw him when I first arrived, which was around seven." *Don't do this, Samantha. Don't withhold information that might lead to finding a missing boy. Protecting him now won't help anybody.* "He argued with Hans," I told Madden. "Probably around 7:15. I'm pretty sure Hans slapped him. I didn't see it, but I heard what sounded like a slap, and the young man's cheek was bright red as if he'd been hit."

"Where did this altercation take place?"

"In the study. With the jeans." I paused for a moment, bit my lip, and then charged forward. "You mentioned some crimes in Philadelphia that involved boys Jameson's age, remember?"

"Yes."

"I went through back issues of the *Philadelphia Post* to find out what those crimes were, and I found a picture of one of the missing boys. In the picture, the boy is standing with his friend Jameson Lestes."

"Cat was angry about that photo. She thinks it put Jameson on someone's radar and he became a target. He went missing not long after that article ran and nobody's heard from him since."

"I don't think he went missing. I think he ran away. I think Jameson might be—"

At that moment, the front door slammed. I whirled around and faced Dante. He was far enough inside that he must have been standing there, must have been listening, must have heard my theory, must have suspected what I'd been about to say. My phone slipped out of my hand and fell to the floor.

Dante strode forward picked it up, then held it out to me. His eyebrows were drawn so low over his eyes, the top half of his deep brown irises were hidden. His lips were a tight line, and his body was coiled with hostility. He didn't need to say a word to convey the message: get off the phone and don't tell Madden anything else.

"Sorry about that," I said into the phone.

"You think Jameson might be what?"

Shoot. My clumsiness hadn't distracted Madden. "In danger," I finished lamely.

"I know," he said. "I'm using every resource I can to help find him."

"Keep me posted." I hung up.

"What did you find out?" Dante demanded.

"No hello? No how are you?"

"Not now."

"Look," I said. I twisted around and pointed to the photo in the paper.

"I know about the photo."

I twisted back. "I saw him. At Braeburn Castle the night of my interview. He has the beginning of a beard, which make him look older than fourteen, but it's him."

Dante squinted. "How sure are you?"

"Pretty sure. Very sure. Sure. I'm sure." He stared at me. "Okay, I can't be one hundred percent sure, but I wouldn't say anything if I thought I was wrong, right? I wouldn't want to get your hopes up."

"What did he tell you?"

"Nothing," I said. "I was on my way back to the club-room when I saw—I think I saw—him and Hans arguing."

There something funny about that, though. I stared at the corner of the room while I reached for the memory of that night. It was harder to retrieve thanks to the benzodiazepine, but something had occurred to me *before* I drank the water.

It came back to me. "They were in a room filled with jeans. And then Hans asked me about jeans." I forgot that Dante didn't know about the Fahrenheit Guild, or my interview, or the benzodiazepine. "During my interview. I said I almost never wear jeans."

"You're wearing jeans now," he said.

I glanced down at the white Levi's. "These don't count. They're from the seventies. They're vintage."

Dante shook off my logic. "How did Hans react to what you said?"

"He didn't seem happy. I got flustered. I drank from the water glass at the vacant seat and then collapsed."

"You collapse a lot," Dante said.

"I was *drugged*," I said. "Benzodiazepine."

"Rohypnol?" I could tell I'd gotten his attention.

"I don't know. Madden hasn't confirmed that's what it was, but that's one of the drugs he mentioned. Does that matter?"

He leaned back against the wall. "One of the abducted boys had a full tox panel. They found traces of Rohypnol in his system."

I remembered how I'd felt when I laid on the floor of the clubroom. I hadn't collapsed so much as I recognized I could no longer stand. My arms and legs had felt like noodles, and the ability to support myself had temporarily left me.

"Why would someone drug those teens and leave them passed out in public parks?"

Dante didn't answer my question. "When was this interview?"

"Two days ago," I said. He nodded and turned to leave. "Where are you going?"

"The castle."

"Wait." I grabbed his arm and turned him toward me. "If Madden hasn't released the crime scene, then you can't get in."

"Find out."

Dante had an agenda backed with urgency. Intellectually, I understood why. But I didn't know why Jameson came to Ribbon or ended up at Braeburn castle. I didn't believe for a second he had a legitimate reason for running away from Dante, but something had spooked him enough to leave Philadelphia and not confide in his mom or aunt.

And then a horrible possibility occurred to me. By calling Madden and telling him about Jameson, I'd made Dante's son a murder suspect. Even worse, maybe Jameson was guilty.

12

IT'S THE CAR

I SHOVED MY PHONE INTO THE VINTAGE MAIL CARRIER BAG and left the newspapers sitting out on the table. Dante's motorcycle was parked behind my Supra. A light rainfall had coated both vehicles. "I'm driving," I said. Dante looked at me as if he planned to protest. I strode toward the driver's side and got in. Dante dropped into the passenger-side seat.

Half a mile away from Dante's apartment, a purple Camaro pulled up next to us, and the driver lowered his window. "What's the torque on that?" he asked Dante.

Dante leaned back and said, "It's for you."

I leaned forward. "Three sixty-eight. Sixteen hundred RPMs." The SUV driver looked surprised. "You know what else? It goes zero to sixty in four-point-four seconds."

He looked at Dante. Dante shrugged. The light changed and I gave the guy a demonstration.

"You're different these days," Dante said. "More confident."

"It's the car."

IT WOULD HAVE MADE sense to call Madden back and find out if he'd released the crime scene, but in my trademark line of reasoning, showing up would possibly net us more information. I didn't know what we might find when we got there, but the one thing I never expected was a second Toyota Supra A91 in Refraction Blue parked in a visitor space out front.

"Matching set?" Dante asked.

I scowled. "They produced a thousand of them in total, and Refraction Blue is supposed to be the most exclusive color. Some bozo in Ribbon had to go out and buy a car like mine?" I thought about every time a random guy talked car specs with me at a traffic light. I'd probably sold more limited edition Toyota Supras than the salesman without even trying!

There was no point taking a space farther from the door to put distance between the two vehicles, and in an aggressive show of boldness, I parked right beside the other one. Dante and I got out and I locked the car via remote. My thumb accidentally hit the panic button, and the alarm went off. My swagger faded, and I fumbled with the key, hitting every button on it until the alarm went silent.

I glared at Dante. "Don't say a word."

In a gesture that evoked the old days, he held both hands up in surrender. "Your problem. Not mine."

We approached the front of the castle. In the broad daylight of the crisp October afternoon, the castle looked almost welcoming. Thick puffs of smoke billowed out of the chimney, comingling with cumulus clouds overhead. Sunrays illuminated the façade, highlighting flecks of green and blue in the otherwise gray stones. I lost a few seconds gazing at the castle keep, imagining Rapunzel and wondering how long she'd had to let her hair grow for it to reach the ground. I shook off the fairy tale and refocused on the reason I was here.

I yanked on the heavy wood door at the exact moment someone pushed it open from inside. The door swung toward me too easily and I stumbled backward into Dante. He was like a wall of muscle. I would have been more embarrassed by the body contact if not for the identity of the man who exited the castle.

"What are you doing here?" I blurted.

Detective Loncar was a mid-sixty-year-old former homicide detective turned retiree turned private investigator. He was the first member of law enforcement I'd encountered after moving back to Ribbon. He'd been a thorn in my side until he became first an ally, then a makeover candidate, and ultimately, a mentor.

On good days, I referred to us as collaborators. (On *really* good days he didn't kick me out of his office for saying it.) (On bad days, I went back to calling him a thorn in my side.)

Loncar seemed as surprised by my presence as I was his. He held a familiar-looking Toyota key fob in his hand, which he aimed at my car.

Oh, no.

No, no, no, no, no.

NO.

"What the—?" he muttered as he stared at the matching vehicles.

"You didn't," I said. I crossed my arms over my chest and shook my head.

"What's that?" His chin jutted toward the two cars, though I could surmise he meant mine, not the other one.

"That?" I pointed to my car. "That is my limited edition Toyota Supra A91 in Refraction Blue. I bought it after solving the pretzel case. I got the feeling from the dealer that it was *rare*."

Detective Loncar—just Loncar to everybody else now that he'd retired—had spent the better part of his life married to a woman who had recently decided to leave him. He hadn't wanted the divorce and after the train left the station without him, he found himself ill-equipped for the single life. I'd used my considerable shopping skills to upgrade his wardrobe, and Nick's dad had lent a hand (and a vacant seat at his weekly poker game). The two men occasionally went out to senior mixers together, which was equal parts charming and frightening. I'd learned not to ask details.

"Do women flirt with you at traffic lights?" Loncar asked.

"No," I said, then quickly added, "I get men who want to talk car specs." And then I remembered the guy who'd said he saw a man driving this car last week. I'd told him it was my husband. Did people think Loncar and I were *married?*

The thought must have occurred to Loncar at the same time it came to me, because he blushed, glanced at me, and then looked away.

"We have to take them out together," I said in a rush.

"Be seen in the same place so people know there are two of them. Otherwise, they'll think…" My voice trailed off so he could put two and two together himself.

"Right." He pocketed his keys and turned back to the door.

As I entered the castle, I considered why Loncar was here in the first place. Back when I was planning his retirement party, he'd gotten shot in the line of duty. Madden had been the officer to handle the case, and I'd seen how he'd remained an outsider amongst Ribbon's police officers. As the baton of detective passed from one man to the other, they must have established a professional friendship of sorts, which now led to outside help on a difficult case.

The interior was cozy. There were no windows directly off the vestibule, and even in daylight, it took a few seconds for my eyes to adjust to the darkness. Movement was visible out of the corner of my eye, and I jumped and then spotted Wilhelm. His mottled fur blended in with the exposed brick wall and Turkish carpets, and I could easily see how he had his run of the place. If we could get the cat to talk, we'd know everything.

I'd lost track of Dante while Loncar and I had our *Fast and Furious* moment out front, but Dante had his methods for investigation, so I didn't mention him now. I led the way to the study and found Lucy packing piles of jeans into boxes.

Today she wore a man's oversized white oxford, like the one she'd worn the night of my interview, over a white tank top, crisp denim jeans, and Gucci loafers. A gold charm bracelet dangled from her wrist. Her blond hair was secured into a low ponytail and tied with a red and white silk scarf.

"Samantha, this is a surprise," she said. She held a large cardboard box and appeared to struggle under its weight. "Can you give me a hand with this?"

"Sure," I said. I glanced behind me at Loncar, but he hadn't followed me into the room. "It's okay to pack these up?" I asked.

"The police made a mess of the room with their fingerprint powder. That Detective Madden said they were done in here. Marguerite did five loads of laundry this morning, but the rest of the room needs a thorough cleaning."

I stepped around the garments on the floor and grabbed the other side of the box. "Where are we taking them?"

"To the storage closet down the hall," she said.

Even with every light on, the study was poorly lit. I brushed against the desk, and black powder transferred onto my white jeans. I tried to swipe it away, and it faded to gray.

"We're foolish to do this while wearing white," Lucy said. "Even after being dusted, there's fingerprint powder everywhere."

I took tentative backward steps out of the room, careful not to trip over any of the piles on the floor, and then allowed Lucy to lead the way until we reached an open, walk-in closet. It was about four feet deep, with chrome baker's racks installed on either side. The shelves were partially filled with neatly stacked piles of jeans like you might find in a store stockroom. "Set it down," she instructed.

We lowered the box to the floor and righted ourselves. Lucy put her hand on her hip and bent forward. "I hate physical labor," she said.

Lucy didn't act like someone who had lost a relative. Still, I said, "I'm sorry for your loss. Hans was," I paused and sought the appropriate word. "It's always sad to lose a family member."

"So, the word is out." She crossed her arms. "I wondered how long it would take. Who told you?"

"I have connections at the paper."

"Great. Family ties—the gift that keeps on giving." She bent down and retrieved a pair of jeans that she'd dropped. "My grandmother died when I was thirty-two. The next year, Hans sought me out. He said he had an affair with her, and I was his granddaughter. I asked for a paternity test and our blood type matched."

It didn't quite match what I'd heard, but facts like this were often distorted by gossip. "That must have been a surprise," I said. "Finding out you're the heir to a small fortune at thirty-two years old."

"Honestly, I wish he never told me."

My first thought was that most people would kill to learn they had Hans's money to look forward to upon his death, but I didn't know how to express that without accusing her of being a gold-digger, a murderer, or both.

"Did you two develop a relationship after that? If he sought you out, it sounds like that's what he wanted."

"What Hans wanted. That's rich. You must not have read the paper today. Hans was a nasty old man who was guilty of war crimes. All his money came from his horrible past. He deserved to die a long time ago, but even Satan didn't want him."

Lucy didn't hide her hostility. I wondered how she'd justify her inheritance now. The promise of wealth, I've found, tends to make it harder to hold a grudge. Would ownership of a castle be enough to soften Lucy's feelings about her grandfather?

We returned to the study and Lucy placed an empty box on the desk. "Can you hand me the stack of jeans by the chair?" she asked.

I picked up the pile and carried it to her. "What are all of these?"

"Hans was the denim expert in the Fahrenheit Guild. This mess is the result of his near-obsession when it came to documenting the history of jeans. He shopped retail to get samples from different countries and factories, he bought deadstock from jobbers, and he rooted through thrift stores to find examples from different eras. There's a room on the other side of the castle where he was going to display a timeline of denim. Cecile thought he wanted to convert the castle into a museum, but when she brought it up at a meeting, he practically bit her head off. I think jeans were so uniquely American to him, they became a symbol of how to blend in after the war."

I'd always thought jeans were jeans. Boot cut, skinny, baggy, boyfriend, flare. Faded or dark wash. That was about the extent of my denim knowledge. I failed Denim 101 thanks to a boyfriend who worked at the local theater, or rather, thanks to the free movie admission I got by dating him. I made up the credits by auditing the course before graduation but put in minimal effort since the grade wouldn't count toward my GPA. When it came time for finals, I'd put all my energy into Early American Designers instead.

"Jeans." I handed Lucy the stack, and she set it in the bottom of the empty carton. "Hans said something about me being his successor. What was his garment?"

"The 1944 Levi's 501. He called it the holy grail of jeans."

"When I asked about the work the guild does, you said you purchase two garments: one for preservation, and one to deconstruct so you can learn every step that went into making it. Did Hans actually deconstruct a pair of jeans from 1944?"

She shrugged. "They were in the archives when I was old enough to join. He said he got them the year he moved to the United States."

I picked up a pair of jeans from the floor and held them by the waistband. They were faded to a shade of blue that was near white in places. The denim was soft from a lifetime of laundry cycles, and whiskers from wear creased the crotch area. The hems of the pants were frayed from dragging on the ground. They weren't all that different from the two pairs of dad jeans I put in my does-not-spark-joy pile last night. I'd probably passed up dozens of jeans like this in thrift stores.

"Can I borrow these?" I asked Lucy. "For research?"

"I don't think that's a good idea," she said. She held out her hand, and I gave them to her.

I watched her fold the faded pair and set them on her stack. "Are the 1944 ones here in the castle?"

"Yes," she said. "They're with the rest of the historical garments. Ahn's up there. If you go now, you'll catch her before she locks up."

I felt a zing as another guild member's name was mentioned. So far, I'd had relatively little interaction with each of the board members, and my interest in their mission temporarily drove the fact that one of them was a suspected murderer from my mind.

I followed Lucy's directions through the castle, past the bar, and into a wing I hadn't previously accessed.

Halfway up the staircase, the thought I'd banished returned. The night Hans was murdered, there'd been a handful of people on the premises. One of them was guilty. This wasn't like other mysteries I'd helped solve where any number of enemies could have gained access and committed the crime. It was a closed-circle mystery. Yet none of them seemed scared for their life. None of the remaining guild members acted as if a murderer was among them or on the loose.

At the end of the hall, a small, curved staircase led to the second floor. I could have easily gotten lost in the castle and probably not found my way out for days. I passed several locked rooms until I reached one with a skeleton key in the lock. I turned the knob and it gave way under my grip. The door swung open, and I found Ahn inside.

Today, Ahn wore an oversized black V-neck sweater over a pair of wide, cropped black pants with large pockets by the calf. Black ankle booties with angular block heels completed the look. Her style reflected Asian influences, though I couldn't pinpoint the designers.

When I entered the room, she looked up, surprised. "Samantha," she said. "I did not know you were in the castle."

The truth was, I had no good reason for coming to the castle today. Below us, enough visitors were exploring the place to make my presence less questionable, and for possibly the first time in my life, I silently welcomed the safety that comes in numbers. "We all left abruptly the night of the meeting. I left something behind in the study."

"What?"

"What what?"

"You weren't required to bring anything to the meeting. What did you leave behind?"

I spoke without thinking. "A pair of jeans." Her eyebrows drew together almost imperceptibly. I added, "I asked Lucy if I could borrow a pair for research." Which wasn't a lie, but it was out of order in the events of the past forty-eight hours.

"Of course," she said. "Assuming your membership is approved, that is a good idea."

Was it? Lucy had just told me it wasn't, and now I didn't know which member to trust.

I'd come upstairs to see the archived clothes, and I said as much to change the subject. "Lucy mentioned that you were up here. Can you show me the 501 archives?"

"Also for research?" she asked. I couldn't read her expression and didn't know if the question was more teasing or accusatory.

"Yes."

She nodded her head once and then turned her back to me and faced a wall of floor-to-ceiling plexiglass panels. The room lacked imagination. White walls and white matching carpeting had erased the personality that existed in the rest of the castle. A white laminate table sat in the center. Ahn slipped on a pair of white gloves and moved a plexiglass panel to the side, revealing large white boxes on shelves. I read the labels from where I stood:

Halston jersey dress, 1971. Nudie suit, 1962. Chanel jersey top and trousers, 1929. Claire McCardell bathing suit, 1944. Dior bar jacket, 1947.

It was a fashion historian's dream.

Ahn extracted a box labeled "Levi's 501, 1944" and carried it to the table.

"Gloves," she said. She pointed at a box that sat on the end of the table.

I pulled on a pair. She nodded when I was done and lifted the lid of the box. Sheets of tissue paper had been layered on top of the garment, and one by one, we lifted them out of the box to reveal the garment inside. The process heightened anticipation, but by the time we'd removed all the paper out of the box, my letdown was worse than a post-pizza carb crash.

The 501 box was empty.

13

LIKE ARCHAEOLOGISTS

"THEY'RE MISSING," AHN SAID. AN EDGE OF PANIC LACED her voice. She turned back toward the shelf as if she'd missed something.

"Maybe Hans took them out of storage," I said. "If I was supposed to be his replacement, he might have had them on hand to show me."

"You don't understand," she said. "Hans treated this pair of jeans like they were made of platinum. They weren't just a garment to him. This room is climate controlled, with museum-grade plexiglass protecting the archival boxes and acid-free tissue paper." She pointed to the door. "An alarm sounds in the study and his bedroom when someone comes in."

Another person might think these security measures were drastic for a room filled with old clothes, but judging from the labels I'd scanned, the contents of this room were worthy of belonging to the Met.

"What about the deconstructed version? Is that stored in here too?"

"No." Ahn led me to the room next to us. It was a replica of the one we'd left. I helped her move the 501 box to the table in the center and we repeated the tissue paper elimination. In this box, we found eighteen pieces of denim each laid flat and sealed in plastic. Four separate vacuum-sealed pouches contained copper rivets, buttons, thread, and a red tab.

This pair of 501s had been taken apart, stitch by stitch, and then preserved by component. Like archeologists assembling a dinosaur skeleton from a dig, we arranged the components of the jeans on the table with minimal space between them until they loosely took on the shape of their original form.

Ahn pulled an inventory sheet out of the box. Her eyes moved back and forth between the box and the piece work on the table. About a minute later, she set the sheet of paper down. "Everything's here but the leather tag," she said.

I studied the makeshift display. To me, there was nothing remarkable about it except for the effort it had taken someone to deconstruct and then seal into protective plastic. I picked up a back pocket and ran my fingers over the stitching. I had an education that put me in the top one percent when it came to fashion history, but I'd never put jeans in the same rarified air as other fashion classics. Now I was out of my element.

I set the pocket down. "What's going to happen to the guild now that Hans is gone?" I asked.

"Nothing," Ahn said. One by one she picked up the piecework and set it back into the box between layers of tissue. "Hans didn't want to step down, but we demanded he find a replacement. You were going to take his place so we could continue."

"Why me?" I asked. "I could see if it was for any other garment, but why me for jeans?" I was about to say I knew next to nothing about them, but a tiny part of me still wanted to gain acceptance to their club, and I didn't want to blow it now.

"We told Hans he had to find someone or we would," Ahn said. "He dragged his feet on it, so Cecile asked around. One of our adjunct members put forth your name."

"Who?"

"I'm sorry. Membership is secret. Hans hated the suggestion, but that made you look better. We put it to a vote and you passed twenty-two to one."

An odd feeling came over me. Knowing everyone but the person I was expected to replace had wanted me as a member. And a new thought came to me. If a guild member had planned to murder Hans, then what better night to do it than the night a stranger was on the premises?

Had I been invited to join because someone needed a scapegoat?

I was getting a clearer picture as to why Hans had greeted me with hostility. He didn't want me there. He didn't agree that it was time to replace him, and he probably would have wanted to choose his successor. It was a powerplay by the rest of the board, and he could have fought them if he wanted. He'd probably secretly wished I had car trouble or some other equally flakey excuse to show up late or not at all.

He might have even wanted me out of the picture.

My memory of that first night fluttered back, and I asked Ahn a question that had been on my mind. "Five people were conducting my interview. You, Buck, Hans, Cecile, and Lucy." I ticked the names off on my fingers as I listed them. "But there were six glasses of water set up. Who was the one on the end for? Did someone not show?"

"We told the staff to provide six glasses. One for each of us and one for you."

I didn't like what that said about the guild, but I had to think more about it before I knew why.

We finished packing the deconstructed 501 into its box then replaced the lid and put the box back on the shelf.

Lucy called up the staircase. "Breaktime is over," she said. "That study won't organize itself."

"We need to tell her about the missing jeans," I said. "Don't we?"

"The archives are not your concern," Ahn said. The dismissal felt pointed, delineating the difference between members and me. Ahn swept her glossy hair off her shoulders and continued in a softer voice. "The archives are unilaterally owned by the guild. No member oversees them." And then she smiled. "Your presence here is as a guest of the board. If it pleases you to tell her then do so, though I would treat it as conversation, not cause for alarm."

"Sure," I said. While nothing she'd said was incorrect, I had the distinct feeling I'd been told to mind my place and not overstep boundaries. She might as well have told me I was Jane Wiedlin's character in the movie *Clue*: the singing telegram who shows up in act two and dies in act three.

It could have been worse. I always dreamed of being a member of The Go-Go's.

We left our gloves in a tray inside the door. I followed Ahn back downstairs, unsure how I felt about our interaction. She was right about one thing: I was a nobody here. I had no experience with their methods for archiving garments, or what circumstances would allow a member to check them out. Ahn seemed unconcerned by what I'd initially thought was a theft, and comparatively speaking, missing jeans were far less problematic than murder.

We came out by the clubroom where my interview had taken place. I imagined the castle like a labyrinth, with stairs and closets and intersecting hallways, and probably even a secret dwelling underneath us, not unlike the Batcave. Ahn pulled on red leather gloves and picked up a black handbag. She removed a set of keys.

"Good luck with your research, Samantha," she said. She left me alone in the hallway.

Ahn was the most reserved member of the Fahrenheit Guild board, and she'd been the most difficult to read. She hadn't gone out of her way to convince me not to share our findings with Lucy, but by dissuading me, she'd all but waved a red flag in that direction. To file under "what could it hurt?" I went in search of Lucy, prepared to gauge her reaction.

When I reached the study, Wilhelm was sleeping on a pile of unfolded jeans. He had his hind legs tucked underneath him and his head resting on his front paws. Lucy stood in the doorway with her hands on her hips and sighed.

"The never-ending storage project. I've got half a mind to have the staff donate them all to a local charity."

"Speaking of the staff, why isn't anyone helping you? This isn't a one-person job."

"Divide and conqueror," she said. "Marguerite's been busy with the laundry. Aside from the detectives who were poking around earlier, it's us and the cat."

"Ahn was here," I said.

"Ahn has never believed that jeans should be part of the guild mission. To her, this," she said, gesturing in an all-encompassing manner toward the stacks of denim, "is garbage."

"How did Hans take that?"

"Not well. There was an argument and he threatened to destroy the kimonos she contributed to the archives. He called them dirty rags—there was a racial slur in there, too, but I prefer not to repeat it. It got ugly, but Hans could be an ugly man."

"And Ahn?"

"She left. We didn't hear from her for over a month, and the board started discussing whether we should replace her or vote on a new garment for inclusion in the archives. She surprised us all when she came back."

"Did she say where she went?"

"No. All she said was that what she honored by being a member of the guild was more important than the insults of a racist. But she wasn't the same. It was as if she'd been lobotomized. We'd had the beginnings of a friendship, but after that she retreated."

"Did you consider kicking Hans out?"

"Hans started the guild. The archives are here at his

castle. He filed the paperwork, put everything in his name, and had the final say on everything we did."

"Except voting. Ahn said I was voted as a nominee twenty-one to one."

"That was for your nomination. If Hans wanted to keep you out, he could have."

Everything Lucy said made Ahn look suspicious, but the information had been shared too freely. Lucy's willingness to spill gossip with very little prodding felt suspicious as if she might be the one with something to hide.

Before I could think more about it, Wilhelm raised his head and blinked a few times. He stretched his front paws and yawned a massive cat yawn that showed us the pink interior of his mouth. He stood, sniffed the jeans he'd made his temporary bed, and jumped down. He brushed his back against the pant leg of my jeans and stalked out of the room.

"What's going to happen to Wilhelm now? You're not going to leave him to fend for himself, are you?"

She chuckled. "Wilhelm can probably fend for himself better than any of us, but no. Marguerite will make sure he has food and water and a clean litterbox. There's the gardener and the landscaper and the cleaning staff. They've worked for Hans for decades, and I assured them that won't change. Wilhelm will still have friends."

"What about the guy who was here the other night?" I asked. "What's his job?"

"What guy?"

"Young man. Red hair and beard scruff. He was in the study the night of my interview. He looked too young to have worked here for long."

Lucy cocked her head to the side. Her lips pursed like

she was running her tongue over her teeth inside her mouth, and the act made her cheekbones stand out by default.

"The detective asked about him too," she said finally. "That's what's so odd. Nobody who works here fits that description."

14

AN ALMOST PREDICTABLE EFFECT

I'D BEEN SO FOCUSED ON WHAT I'D LEARNED ABOUT AHN that it took me a moment to realize what Lucy's statement implied. Nothing about the redhead I strongly suspected was Dante's son said "thief," "malicious intent," or "murderer," but a man had died the night I'd seen him. Once again, I was conflicted; my insistence that there had been another person at the scene of the crime would do more harm for him than good.

Lucy brushed at a smudge of black on her white broadcloth shirt. "Did you tell the police about him?" she asked.

"I don't remember," I lied. "I was still foggy from having collapsed during my interview, and I think my statement probably didn't make a lot of sense."

"Right," she said slowly, then added, "of course. Honestly, Samantha, if you hadn't passed out first, my first thought would have been that *you* were the killer." She put her hand on the doorknob and blocked my exit from the room. "I'm going to go check on the kitchen staff," she said. "That detective got here a while ago and I want to make sure he's not harassing them."

I thought it more likely that Loncar and Dante were sharing notes, but Lucy hadn't seen me arrive, which meant she didn't know Dante was here. The good thing about a guy like Dante was that he'd have an almost predictable effect on a woman like Lucy, which would buy me some snooping time.

"Can I stay and tidy up a bit?" I asked. At her curious expression, I added, "I recently learned a new folding technique. These jeans will take up half the space in your storage closet."

She opened the door back up. "Have at it," she said. "The more you do, the less left for me."

I lost track of time while practicing the Zen of folding. Marie Kondo said folding was a form of dialogue with our wardrobes. If that were true, then the clothes in this room could tell me what happened the night of Hans's death.

I tried to reason things out, but there were too many possibilities. All I really knew was a ninety-five-year-old former German soldier who had come to the United States after World War II and specialized in the history of denim had been found dead under a pile of abandoned inventory.

I shook out a pair of jeans and looked at them. "What can you tell me?" I asked them. (Marie advised talking to our clothes.)

The jeans did not respond. I turned them around and stared at the back pockets. This pair was Wranglers. The stitching on the back pockets had a western flair, a cursive, stylized "W." I folded them with the fly facing in and lay them on the clean surface of the desk. I smoothed the creases out with my hands, and then folded the hems up to about halfway, the waistband down to about halfway, and then folded that in half again. I was left with a neat square of denim. I set them aside and moved on to the next pair. Each time I shook a pair of jeans open and asked, "what can you tell me?" and each time, the jeans were silent. I adjusted my question to "did you see anything suspicious?" and eventually "is there anything you'd like me to know?" Despite my careful prodding, Marie's advice to converse with garments continued to be a one-sided effort.

I'd have to consult Dante's book later. Maybe I wasn't doing it right.

I sorted the jeans into piles. Wranglers in one, Lee in another, Levi's in a third, and Designer in a fourth. A fifth stack that remained unfolded was of cheaply made pairs loaded with stretch. It hadn't taken me long to feel the difference between the fabrics in the room, but once I did, I knew the heavier denim was preferable. Even the pairs that were worn and faded had a luxurious feel that the chemically aged ones did not. I'd given a speech about fast fashion the night of my interview, but I'd started to realize that all denim didn't fit into that category.

I finished folding the jeans alongside the bookshelves and stepped out from behind the desk to enter the hallway. According to the grandfather clock at the end of the hall, I'd been at it for hours. The castle was quiet, but that probably had more to do with brick walls and sound-absorbing carpets and tapestries than a lack of activity. I went to the front of the building and peeked my head outside. The sun was setting, and the lingering evening light cast the grounds in shadows. One Toyota Supra was parked out front, and a note was tucked under the windshield. I propped the front door open with a small cast iron turtle and retrieved the note. It said, *Left in the other Batmobile. Touch base later.*

I let myself back inside and went in the direction of the bar. Lucy sat alone with a tumbler of bourbon. The bottle, less than half full, sat to her right next to her cell phone. The screen was lit, as if she'd used it and it hadn't yet slipped into sleep mode.

I cleared my throat and she looked over her shoulder. "Hey, Samantha," she said. She leaned over the bar and pulled up an empty glass. "Want some?"

"No, thanks," I said. She pushed the glass away clumsily and it slid a few inches down the highly polished wood surface.

"Suit yourself." She took another sip and then turned back. Her eyes were bloodshot. "Are you leaving me too?"

"It's closing in on six," I said. "It'll be dark soon."

She shrugged. "Sleep over. We could have a slumber party. Stay up all night, talk about boys, pretend we're teenagers in a haunted castle." She leaned forward. "Maybe Hans's ghost will appear. Wooooooooooo," she finished. Her glass was in one hand, and she held both up when she made the ghost noise. Bourbon sloshed from the tumbler and landed on her shirt. She cursed and swiped at the spot, making it bigger.

"You're not going to sleep here, are you?" I asked. Recognizing that my question was loaded with judgment, I rephrased it. "Do you sleep here often?"

"It's my house now," she said. "Or it will be when probate ends. All of this is now mine. The rumors, the innuendo, and the sordid past that will inevitably attach itself to my name after the reporters who keep calling write their exposés."

I couldn't tell her it wasn't true. I couldn't deny the facts about Hans would make the papers, nor promise that her relationship to Hans would remain a secret.

"What about your parents?"

"They died when I was ten. Heart attacks, two weeks apart. I remember sitting in my bed hoping I'd have one too." She turned her back on me but left her glass untouched. "Go ahead and leave. It's what people do."

I felt the pull of manipulation fed by my innate desire to help. Lucy, I felt, should not be alone tonight. But this wasn't my home, and she wasn't a close friend. For a descendant of one of Ribbon's wealthiest families, she cut a tragic figure. But the possibility remained that she knew more about her grandfather's murder than she let on, and what I saw now was an act.

I left the bar, proud that my legs had taken the common-sense instruction from my brain to leave and not defied it to offer companionship. I was eager to get home. I returned to the study for my handbag. It was on the sofa, buried under a pile of jeans that had tipped over.

That struck me as odd. I'd taken great care with my newly practiced folding skills, and I hadn't bumped into any piles on the way out. Without moving from where I stood, I turned my head slowly and scanned the rest of the room. Something felt different, but I couldn't place what it was. My eyes lingered on the jeans on the floor that I hadn't yet gotten to, the mound of cheap jeans that didn't seem worth my efforts, and the neat stacks that I'd placed by the bookcase.

It felt like a mind game: look at this photo and identify what's wrong. I felt what I imagined a detective would feel when first seeing a crime scene. But if there was a clue here, the police would have found it. Madden and company had been over the castle, left behind fingerprint powder and chaos, taken their pictures, and collected whatever they'd deemed suspicious. I'd spent the past several hours in this room, and if something felt off, it was because something had changed since I'd left.

I glanced at the spines of the books on the shelves. Black fingerprint powder still clung to them, coating the titles, and damaging the spines. I glanced around for a dust rag but seeing none, plucked a handful of tissues out of the box on the desk. I gently wiped over the books to remove the residual powder. Particles fluttered into the air, and I coughed. The short amount of time I'd spent in here had left my outfit filthy.

I was about to chalk my sense of unease up to my imagination when I noticed something that hadn't been in the room before. It was a clue that would disappear before it had the chance to be noticed.

A ring of water from the base of a mug on the glass top surface of the desk.

I'd spent half the day using that very surface as my folding table. If it had been wet, I would have noticed. That meant one thing: someone had been in here after I left.

15

CONCERNED CITIZEN

FEW THINGS MOTIVATE A PERSON TO LEAVE A CREEPY CASTLE after dark more than the notion that they're not alone, and I was no exception. I grabbed my handbag and spun around, all but running toward the front door. It wasn't until I was safely in my car that I remembered Lucy alone in the bar.

Of all the people I thought to call in a moment like this, I chose the most reliable.

"Loncar," the detective answered.

"It's Samantha Kidd," I said. "I don't want to talk about the car." He grunted. "I'm outside Braeburn Castle. There's someone inside. Two someones. Lucy Francis and someone else."

"Ms. Francis has every right to be there, and as the owner, she can entertain whoever she pleases."

"No, it's not like that. I was folding in the study all day, and when I came back, I saw a water ring on the desk. Someone was in the room where Hans was killed."

"You said you were there all day."

"I was at the *castle* all day. Not all day. I went to Dante's apartment first, and then I went to the castle. I was in the study, and then in the storage room, and then upstairs in the archives, and then back to the study, and then the bar, and then the study again." I paused for a moment and ran through each of those rooms in my mind. "Yes. That's where I was all day."

"Where are you now?"

"In my car. If there's someone else in there and Lucy doesn't know, then she could be in danger."

"I admire your concern for your friend—"

"She's not my friend. I barely know her."

"I admire your concern for a woman you barely know, but there isn't a lot I can do."

"There has to be *something*," I said. "I know you're not a cop anymore, but you can do things regular people can't. Can you come over here and check on her? I know! Make up a lame reason, and she'll think you're interested."

Loncar didn't say anything, but I waited his silence out. He was either considering the genius behind my suggestion or pinching the bridge of his nose while he counted to ten. I felt optimistic.

"Ms. Kidd. Is there anything outside the castle that makes you think there's a threat present inside? Another car, a bobbing candle flickering around the lawn, a wolf howling at the moon?"

"Don't mock me," I said. "I'm a concerned citizen, and this castle was the site of a recent homicide. And it's creepy." A flash of lightning lit up the sky, followed by the clap of thunder a few seconds later. "Did you hear that?

That's thunder. It's a sign. This castle is like the house on haunted hill."

"Lock your doors. Stay there until I arrive. When I pull in, you leave. Got it?"

"Got it."

"Give me twenty minutes."

True to his word, he pulled into the castle driveway about twenty minutes later. I recognized the headlights. Perhaps this was an unforeseen side benefit of us owning the same car: we could tag-team stakeouts and confuse perps. I made a mental note to float the suggestion to him when we weren't on a mission.

He pulled up next to me and nodded. I nodded back, started my car, and backed out of my space. By the time I left the premises, he was already inside.

I arrived home to an unlikely scene. Nick, Dante, Detective Madden, and my friend Eddie were seated around the dining room table. A fifth chair was pushed away from the table with a coffee mug on the placemat.

I pointed to the empty seat. "Whose seat is that?"

"Loncar," Nick said. "He was here when you called."

The air in the kitchen was tense. I could count on one hand the number of times Nick and Dante had occupied the same space, and it would take half the fingers of a peace sign to count the times they'd cooperated. Madden's presence made me think this was about Dante's son, and Eddie, well, Eddie might have shown up by accident and gotten caught in the net.

"Dude," Eddie said.

Eddie was, arguably, my closest friend in the world. We'd gone to high school together, lost touch for over a decade, and reconnected when I moved back to my old hometown. Where my style encompassed impractical and eclectic inspirations, Eddie favored message T-shirts and paint-stained canvas trousers. Tonight, he wore a navy blue sweatshirt that said SURELY NOT EVERYBODY WAS KUNG FU FIGHTING.

Eddie was gifted with a creative streak that eventually landed him the job of visual director for a local department store until the store went out of business. After a mind-clearing vacation to Key West, he'd returned and gone freelance, which gave him the same schedule as I had with double the stress. He'd been busy with Halloween decorations for the city for the past few weeks, and our interactions had been limited to coffee and pizza, which, now that I thought about it, wasn't all that different than before he got the job.

Eddie could infuse the word "dude" with any number of emotions, and tonight, it felt heavy. I'd been cautioned to keep the Fahrenheit Guild invitation quiet, and while I had every intention of telling Eddie about it I hadn't wanted to jinx the possibility until it was official. The irony wasn't lost on me now.

"Has there been any news?" I asked. I quickly looked at the faces around the table.

"No," Dante said. "I talked to Jameson's mother earlier today. She spoke to the police but they say he doesn't fit the profile of the other crimes. She claims they didn't fight, but the police seem to think Jameson ran away. He's underage, so that puts him in a different category than an adult."

Dante looked weathered. Sun and a lack of sleep had

left behind lines around his eyes that were deeper than I remembered them being, and the flirtatious glimmer I was used to seeing was dim. While others in the room had coffee mugs in front of them, Dante's placemat held a collection of beer bottles. On a good day, Dante was rough around the edges, like Brando in *The Wild One.* Tonight, he was more *On the Waterfront.*

As I stood in my kitchen, assessing the group in front of me, I was suddenly sure of one thing: I couldn't *not* tell them what I suspected. Dante was at my table, and that couldn't be because he'd dropped by unannounced while I was at the castle. He knew Nick lived here with me. And Detective Madden had been the one to tell me about the missing boy in the first place. He cared about Cat. He would want to see Jameson found.

"I think Jameson is living at the castle," I said. "I met a guy the first night I was there." I pulled the torn piece of newspaper out of my back pocket and set it on the table. "I think that's him in the picture. That's how I recognized him. But when I asked Lucy about him, she said there's nobody like him working there."

"You have a theory," Nick said.

Our eyes connected. He knew me well enough to know how my mind worked. I suspected everyone of everything until the pieces in front of me fit the picture in my mind. Nick and Loncar consistently tried to steer me away from investigating for wildly different reasons. Loncar wasn't here, and Nick, if I were reading his expression right, wasn't going to tell me to stop.

"I have a theory." I stared at Nick until he nodded his encouragement and then I continued. "I think Jameson saw who killed Hans. I think he was in the study, maybe hiding behind the desk, and he knows who did it, but because he's on the run himself, he didn't do anything to stop the crime from happening, and now he might be hanging around to make sure the guilty person gets caught."

16

JEAN JACKED

"WHAT EVIDENCE DO YOU HAVE?" MADDEN ASKED. IT WAS an entirely legitimate question coming from a detective, and I hoped he'd appreciate my answer.

"None. That's why I didn't tell you any of this when you questioned me. This is all conjecture. Jameson could have hitchhiked up to Canada, down to Florida, or west to California. I don't know him, so I don't know how he makes his decisions or what motivated him to leave in the first place."

Madden leaned back and drummed his fingers on the table. I stared at them while they thrummed out a beat. *Badarabum. Badarabum. Badarabum.*

Loncar had a similar habit that, the first time I'd found myself face to face with him, had driven me nuts. He'd tapped his hand with his wedding ring against the wooden arm of his chair. *Tap tap tap.* He'd bounced the eraser side of a pencil against his desk blotter. *Bounce bounce bounce.* He'd drum his fingers or tap his thigh or spin his wedding ring (before his divorce; now he reached for his ring finger and seemed surprised to find it bare). He used these mindless patterns of noise while he thought, not even noticing that he did it. And now Madden did it too.

Finally, Madden broke the silence. "I spoke to a friend in the Philadelphia police department. He said there's a detail about three of the recent abductions they haven't released to the public. They don't know if it's important. The boys were all wearing jeans the night they were found."

"How do the police know?" I asked. "Don't tell me the boys posted selfies on social media."

"In trying to find a pattern, the police requisitioned the victims' cell phone records. Through location services, they pinpointed the victims' activity before the abductions and accessed traffic and security cameras in the area. They might never have put it together if the boys hadn't been found in their underwear."

"You think they were jean-jacked?" I asked.

"It's difficult to say if taking the jeans bought the abductor some time or if jeans acquisition was the goal all along."

My stomach turned. This case came with a healthy side of nausea. "Did these cameras catch a crime being committed?"

"No," he said. "In each case, the victim woke in an area out of view of a camera."

"That can't be a coincidence," I said.

Madden nodded. "Coincidence does seem an unlikely explanation."

I'd been tangentially and close-up involved in multiple murder investigations in recent years, but the common denominator between them was that they'd been crimes of passion. Love, greed, revenge, betrayal. This sounded like something different.

"What do you know about the Fahrenheit Guild?" I asked the group.

"They're a secret fashion society that memorizes the construction of famous classic garments and passes them down to new generations," Eddie said. "Hans founded them in nineteen fifty-four after reading Ray Bradbury's book *Fahrenheit 451.* The same concept as the book, except the guild's mission is to preserve fashion patterns, not literature." He glanced at the other faces around the table, ran his hand through his shaggy blond hair, and looked at me. "I'm an adjunct member. I knew if I told you about it you'd want to join, but there wasn't anything you could do until one of them died or retired." He smiled a wry smile. "I guess someone died or retired."

I'd never suspected Eddie had been behind my nomination, but it made sense. "What's your garment?"

"Checkered Vans. Style #98. Accessories aren't given the same membership benefits as garments."

"Why weren't you there the night of my interview?"

"Sponsors can't be present when their nominees are interviewed. It would send a message of support, and the board makes it clear that decisions are made based on their approval."

Nick went into the kitchen. He pulled a fresh coffee mug out of the cabinet and carried it to the table with the pot of coffee. He set the mug in front of the seat Loncar had vacated and filled it, then topped off Eddie and Madden's mugs. Dante shook his head.

"Hans Braeburn had a passion for jeans," I said. I'd

been standing all this time, but we were getting somewhere, and perhaps Loncar and I could tag-team this too. "He memorized the 1944 Levi's 501. He has a whole study filled with jeans. I spent hours folding them today."

Dante raised his eyebrows on the word "folding," and Nick looked like he was about to say something and thought better of it. I continued. "Ahn, one of the board members, was going to show me the archives, but the 501 was missing."

"Not possible," Eddie said. "Those rooms are locked, temperature-controlled, and motion-monitored."

"Right," I said. "But the jeans weren't in their box. I saw that myself. And Ahn was as surprised as I was."

"Who has access to the archives?" Madden asked Eddie.

"Board members," Eddie replied.

"What did Ahn do when she saw the empty box?" Madden asked me.

"Nothing," I said. "I thought it was suspicious. She said members have the autonomy to remove samples if they want. We replaced the tissue paper and went to the next room where the deconstructed jeans were kept. We unpacked that one, and she showed me how they vacuum-sealed the individual components. We laid them out like a dinosaur skeleton, and then put the piecework back into the box."

"Fingerprints?" Nick said hopefully.

"Gloves," Eddie and I said at the same time.

Dante, who'd been quiet while I spoke, leaned forward. "Why did you call Loncar?"

I told them about Lucy drinking alone at the bar. I told them about her hostility toward Hans and her off-the-cuff invitation that I spend the night. I told them about the tipped stack of jeans by the door to the study and the water ring on the glass-top desk inside.

Dante pushed his chair away from the table. "I'm going back," he said. "If Jameson's hiding out there, he's in danger."

"Loncar is already there."

"Loncar will need backup. Let's go." He pulled on his black leather motorcycle jacket and left the chair pushed away from the table.

"Samantha isn't leaving," Madden said. I agreed with him, but he was the last person I expected to protest on my behalf, and I wanted to know why. "I need to talk to her alone."

Dante seemed unfazed by Madden's instructions. He held out his hand. "Give me your keys."

We held stares for a long, tense moment. I dropped my eyes to Nick's, and then shifted them from his eyes to the three empty beer bottles that sat at Dante's place and back to Nick's. He pushed his chair away from the table. "I'll drive," he said.

Eddie's eyes widened. A moment later, he stood up too. "I'm coming with."

I guess we'd been thinking the same thing.

Detective Madden and I stayed behind while Dante, Nick, and Eddie left. I understood Dante's need to do something and appreciated Nick's offer to help. Those two would never be friends, but it took extreme circumstances to pull opposing forces together. I couldn't think of anything more extreme than the feeling that your child was in peril.

Eddie, I'd determined, was destined for sainthood.

After the front door closed behind the three men, I turned back to Madden.

"I can't go with them," he said. "I have to follow procedure. Everything I've learned tonight is conjecture, and I need to follow protocol so I don't jeopardize the case. I'm here as moral support."

There was a secondary reason Madden couldn't go, but neither of us said it. If Jameson was there, he'd need to be questioned about the night Hans was murdered. I couldn't deny the thought that he might have been involved. Madden, as the lead detective on the case, wouldn't be able to ignore that fact because his girlfriend's brother was the boy's dad.

"How well do you know Jameson?" I asked. "I've never met him," I added.

"He's a good kid, but he's at an age where he could benefit from a positive role model."

"You mentioned that before. Did something happen?"

"He got into some trouble over the summer. Apparently, he's been hanging with a rough older crowd. There was a brawl, and a couple of kids went to the hospital. Jameson came home with a black eye and bruised ribs, but he wouldn't tell his mom what happened. After the police showed up at her door, she called Dante and said it was his turn."

"Cat told you all this?" I asked.

He nodded. "She was worried about the situation. She loved Jameson, and he was great with her baby. But Jameson and Dante didn't have a typical father-son relationship, and if Dante were suddenly thrust into the role of authority figure, it would have changed things."

"Was Dante a good dad?"

"He's a natural," he said. He took a sip of his coffee and then added, "Nick will be a good dad too."

I smiled. "Someday," I said.

It was one subject Nick and I had stopped talking about, but as my fortieth birthday came and went, it was as if an amplifier had been hooked up to my biological clock. Nick had always wanted kids. I liked them in theory but was scared by the probability of failure as a parent. I sometimes worried my fear would be the thing that pulled me and Nick apart.

As if on cue, Logan entered the kitchen. As far as babies went, he was more my speed. He hopped up onto Eddie's seat, put his front paws on the table, and sniffed the mug of coffee. He dunked his paw in and licked it, and then shook his head and made a spitting sound.

I picked Logan up and shifted him to my lap. He nosed against my arm while I scratched his ears. I felt his feline body relax, and then he lowered himself and curled up on my thighs.

"Samantha, I'm glad everybody left us alone. There's something I need to talk about to you."

"Is it Cat? How's that going? It seems like you two are getting close."

"Cat's fantastic." He indulged in a warm smile. "You should see her with her baby. She lights up the room when she holds her."

"Do you think you two—" I stopped. Whether or not Madden and Cat had a future more permanent than dating was none of my business.

"My intentions are honorable," he said.

This was what I liked the most about Madden. He had a way of acting like a gentleman without evoking outdated gender roles. I couldn't think of anyone who'd make a better partner for my friend.

"I trust you," I said. "But if it's not about Cat, then what did you want to talk about?"

"Remember the night of the murder? When you gave me your statement, you handed me a bag containing a urine sample."

I felt the flush of embarrassment. It's not every day you hand off a mixed nuts jar filled with pee to your friend's boyfriend, but somehow, with everything that had happened of late, I'd forgotten all about that.

"I told Patti to put it in storage and do a blood workup on Mr. Braeburn. She found traces of a benzodiazepine in his blood. On a hunch, she ran analyzed your sample and found the same thing. Whoever slipped the drug into your water probably intended it for him. It widens the scope of the possible murderer because if Mr. Braeburn was temporarily paralyzed from the suppressive effects of the drug, almost anyone could have overpowered him. But Patti found something else."

"Another clue?"

"Not exactly," he said. "She told me you're pregnant."

THE HUMAN MIND

WHATEVER HEAT HAD COLORED MY FACE AT THE REMINDER of my jar of pee now vanished, leaving my arms and legs cold and tingly. I put my hands on Logan and held him in place. He flinched. I kept my hands on his fur, and his even breathing returned as he relaxed. I concentrated on the rhythmic pattern until my heart rate fell into sync.

"She's sure?" I asked. "Those tests sometimes make mistakes."

"She's a coroner, not a gynecologist. I'd get a second opinion, but that's me."

A jumble of emotions overcame me. I reached for my coffee mug and then thought better of it. Logan had me pinned into my seat. Madden got up and filled a glass of water, then carried it to the table.

"The drugs—the benzodiazepines." I put my hand on my abdomen. "Are there side effects?"

"There's risk," he said. "Your doctor can tell you more."

"Who else knows?"

"Me, you, and a woman who spends her time around

dead people. This isn't my business. I have no intention of telling Cat or Dante."

I drank the glass of water. I knew one thing: I wanted Nick to get home.

Logan seemed to sense my anxiety. He raised his head and yawned, stretched out his front paws, and then stood and moved onto Eddie's vacant seat. He sniffed the cushion, and then hopped down and helped himself to water from his bowl.

Freed from lap duty, I stood up and cleared the abandoned mugs from the table. My mind was swimming with questions and concerns, fears, and fantasies. I'd run into countless dangerous situations in the past, motivated by a desire to help save a friend over concern for my safety. But for the first time, it dawned on me that what happened to me would happen to this little life inside me.

It also dawned on me that the person who'd drugged me had put that little life in danger.

I finished cleaning the kitchen and joined Madden in the living room. "You don't have to stay," I said. "I appreciate it, but I'll be okay."

"If you don't mind, I'd like to be here when the others get back. There might be an update to the situation."

Without spelling it out, I understood. Regardless of whether Dante and Madden got along with each other, Dante wouldn't seek out Madden as a confidante regarding Jameson, not while Jameson was tied to an open homicide investigation. Madden's best chance at staying in the loop was to be around when information was exchanged. He was in a difficult situation for more than one reason and I didn't envy him.

We moved from the kitchen into the living room. I sat

on the sofa and Madden took the wingback chair by the front door. "How much do you know about the human mind?" he asked.

It wasn't a question I'd expected, but I welcomed the surprise shift in conversation. "I know a little about creating neuropathways and reprogramming limiting beliefs. Why?"

He looked at me as if confused, and then looked away and blinked a few times. He appeared to be deep in thought. Nick had had a similar reaction when I first started talking about neuropathways, but after I installed a subliminal messaging program on his computer that trained him to believe everything I said, things were smooth sailing.

"Witness statements are often unreliable, and the more a witness is asked to recount an event, the more inaccurate information will creep in. It isn't that a witness is lying, but that the brain has a natural desire to fill in narrative gaps. If a witness remembers two separate moments from an account, they are likely to invent what they believe connects the two without ever recognizing that this piece of information is fabricated."

"This *isn't* about neuropathways," I clarified.

"No. I took your statement the night of Mr. Braeburn's murder. If I ask you about that night again, the chances are high that any new information you recall will be unreliable. You've been back to the castle, and your subconscious has had a chance to try to make sense of the evening."

"If you already took my statement, then why worry?"

"We collected the empty glasses from the clubroom

and found traces of benzodiazepine in the two glasses on either end of the table."

"What about the rest of the glasses?"

"One had traces of whiskey, and two were untouched."

"And the third?"

"Empty with no trace of poison."

"If Hans always sat at the end of the table and someone wanted to poison him, but didn't know *which* end he would choose, they might put poison in two glasses and place them at opposite ends," I said.

"Yes."

"Buck Hollinger had a flask," I said. "During my interview. He unscrewed it and poured the contents into his water glass. I didn't think anything of it, but if he knew the water was tainted, he'd have a good reason for bringing his own beverage."

Madden nodded. "He told us that in his statement and gave us his flask to test."

"Bourbon?"

"Rye."

"When the maid came in to refill the glasses from the pitcher, Cecile put her hand over her glass. And what about Ahn? She didn't drink the water. Her glass sat untouched. If she knew the pitcher to be tainted, she might avoid it even though she wasn't sitting on the end."

"The pitcher wasn't tainted," Madden said. "We tested it. The drugs were found in Hans's glass and yours."

I didn't know what to make of that. It appeared, at first glance, that someone intended to murder Hans all along and used the excuse of my interview as the opportunity. I didn't know if the voting members had chosen their seats at random, but if they had, it would have been much more difficult to make sure one of them ended up with a glass containing a paralytic drug.

But then why drug me? Lucy claimed that glass was for me all along, which made it seem like someone intentionally drugged me. Maybe it hadn't been an accident, though the person at that table who seemed to want me out of the room was the person I was expected to replace.

I floated this theory to Madden. "The thing that connects me to Hans is that I was there to take his position. His garment was the 1944 501 and they're missing from the archives. That doesn't seem coincidental. What if this isn't about Hans or anything he's done, but it's about the jeans?"

Madden leaned forward and rested his elbows on his thighs. "You're going to need to give me a solid reason for why someone might murder an old man over a pair of jeans."

I wished I had one.

Our conversation lapsed into silence. My mind was racing with Madden's other news, and I found it hard to remain in the moment. I had an undeniable urge to tidy up the whole house.

"I have to do something," I said.

"I don't think it's a good idea."

"I don't mean the castle. I mean here. I'm going upstairs to fold." I handed him the remote. "Feel free to watch a movie."

IT WAS 11:30 when Nick returned home. Alone. I heard stray dialogue pass between him and Madden. I was halfway through the mound of clothes I'd left in the spare bedroom, having picked up each piece and asked myself if it sparked joy, then set it back down when I couldn't answer the question. I was surrounded by ghosts of fashion past, reminders of where I'd been and what I'd done, relics of a life that was on the brink of change. Eventually, I sat down amidst the discarded pile and closed my eyes, and that's where Nick found me.

"Kidd," he said.

I felt a hand on my arm, gentle but insistent. I opened my eyes and saw him, his dark curly hair, his root-beer-barrel-colored eyes, his familiar smile. He brushed his hand against the side of my face and smiled. It was a different smile than the one I knew. It wasn't the one he flashed when he was feeling flirtatious or the one that accompanied his head shake when I did something he found equal parts charming and frustrating. It wasn't the one he used with colleagues and investors. There was a light behind it, an internal glow that changed his features and hinted at a level of intense satisfaction I'd never known he could achieve while married to me.

Madden must have told him.

I smiled back. I was still groggy from sleep, but I reached my arms forward and pulled Nick down next to me. I nestled my head against his solid chest and he wrapped his arms around me and we stayed like that until morning.

It was the most peaceful night of sleep I'd had in years.

18

IT'S NOT THE WAFFLES

THE NEXT MORNING, AFTER TAKING TURNS WITH SHOULDER massages to work out the kinks in our necks, Nick made me waffles to celebrate our news. I didn't want him to know how nervous I was at the potential change to our future because his happiness was contagious, and a part of me thought nothing that made him this happy could be bad.

"I'm going to postpone my trip to China," he said, handing me the softened butter. "I'm already in contact with three different factories stateside, and if I can work out a production schedule and get the piecework done in one of my Italian factories, I can probably eliminate almost all of my international travel."

"But you love Italy," I said.

"And I'll love going there with you." He kissed my forehead and slid a fresh waffle onto my plate. "But first things first. We can put the crib in our bedroom for the first year, but eventually, we'll need a nursery. There's the attic bedroom, but that seems too far away. Maybe my dad can move in and help us out? Although that could get cramped quickly. I'll start looking for a bigger house." He picked up the coffee pot and then looked at it for a moment. "We have to start buying decaf," he said. "I'll pick some up when I'm out today."

He nervously puttered around the kitchen, unable to stand still, and emotions overwhelmed me. I started to cry. At first, I swiped the tears away so he wouldn't see them, but they quickly became too much to hide.

"What's wrong?" he asked. He came over to me. "Is it the waffles? Are they no good?" He picked up my plate and sniffed them. "I can make a fresh batch. Or would you rather have French toast?"

"It's not the waffles," I said.

"Is it hormones?" he asked nervously. A flash of concern crossed his face.

"I can't do it," I said. I looked up at him through blurry eyes. "I'm always getting involved in crazy situations and you're the calm one and now you're not calm and that means I have to be calm and I can't do that. I can't do calm. You'll have to give up your dreams and I'll screw it up. Everything is going to change." By this point, I was blubbering.

"Oh, Kidd," Nick said. "Come here." He lifted me out of my chair and held me. I gave in to the tears and sobbed against his chest. He stroked my back and whispered in my hair. "Your craziness is what I love about you the most. I don't want you to change. I don't want anything to change. I want you to be you so our baby gets to know the person I fell in love with."

I sniffled. "Maybe we'll have a girl and she'll grow up to be like me," I said.

I felt Nick's body tense. "Maybe," he said. For the first time since we'd acknowledged the news, I heard the nerves I felt reflected in his voice.

After waffles, we took a proper nap in our bed and then woke. I made an appointment with my doctor to make things official. Having absolutely nothing to go on but the faint memory of a passionate night a month and a half ago when I sent Nick off to China, I counted out months on a calendar and drew a star on July.

I'd been so preoccupied with my news for Nick that I hadn't thought about the murder since last night. (It was odd relying on a homicide to restore calm to my emotions, but I am who I am.)

I asked Nick to bring me up to speed on his night with Dante.

"Are you sure you want to talk about that?" he asked.

"I *need* to talk about that. I need things to be a little normal."

"Homicide investigations aren't normal."

"Speak for yourself."

Nick sighed. "Loncar was out front when we got there. He sent Lucy home and was keeping an eye on the castle. Eddie and Dante did a perimeter check to look for signs of something unusual while I talked to Loncar."

"Did they find anything?" I asked.

"Just a cat," Nick said.

"Mottled gray and orange fur?"

Nick nodded.

"That's Wilhelm. He has the run of the place."

"When they finished circling the property, Dante stayed behind with Loncar. I brought Eddie back here and he drove home. I didn't expect to find Madden alone in the living room, but when he told me what he told you, I was happy he hadn't left you alone."

"Madden is a good guy," I said. "I think things are going well with him and Cat. Maybe she'll move back to Ribbon soon."

When Cat's husband died, she was eight months pregnant. She sold her local boutique and moved to Philadelphia to be closer to family while she raised the baby. It was her husband's murder that first introduced Cat and Detective Madden, though I hadn't known about his interest in her until over a year later.

"You should visit her," Nick said. "She can probably give you some advice."

Nick was right, and I knew he was right, but Cat wasn't like me. Dante was.

I was freaking out about the possibility that I'd be responsible for a life, and Dante was responsible for a life. He'd been as involved as his ex-girlfriend had let him be, and that had been enough...until one day she'd needed more. That day was the day his son disappeared. The weight of that fact must be crushing him.

I dressed in an ivory T-shirt and a pair of my dad's jeans that I'd relegated to the does-not-spark-joy pile (I wanted to make sure), kissed Nick goodbye, and left. I pulled on socks and cream alligator-stamped booties that zipped up the back, added a multistrand pearl necklace, and went downstairs. I cleaned up the mess in the kitchen, then pulled on a long, boxy, unlined cream tweed jacket with frayed edges, grabbed my keys, and left.

I followed the increasingly familiar directions to Dante's apartment. I chose not to call him first, on the off chance he'd either not be there or tell me not to come. It could go either way.

He was there, or at least his motorcycle was. Flames were painted on the tank and along the body, similar in style to the flames that were tattooed on his wrists and snaked halfway up his forearms. When most people looked at Dante, they saw a tough biker, rough around the edges. I knew he'd graduated from art school, spent time working for a private investigator, and had a soft side he most frequently indulged when it came to his sister. He smelled like black leather and cinnamon and could probably kill a man with his thumbs. (I added that last part to see if you were paying attention.)

The bad thing about visiting a person who lived on a hillside is that they know you're coming long before you reach their front door. He opened his when I was on step number twenty.

"Took you long enough," he said.

"I had a busy morning."

I'd slept most of the night on a pile of discarded clothes, but Dante's night appeared to have been less restful. Last night, he'd looked exhausted and rough. Today he looked downright dirty.

The normally neat interior of his apartment was messy. The futon was pulled out and his sheets were a jumble. A collection of beer bottles sat on the end table, and a few more sat in the kitchen. The newspapers I'd left out were still there, though pushed back to make room for a plate that held traces of a meal.

The place didn't smell like black leather and cinnamon.

He reached out for my hand and pulled me toward

him. I wasn't expecting that. His hands were on my waist and then moved up toward less available-to-everyone areas. I put my hands on his chest and pushed him away. "Don't do that," I said.

"I won't tell if you don't." He buried his face in my neck.

There was zero conflict in me. I felt like I knew Dante well, and this wasn't the man who'd once loaned out that futon to me when I needed an escape. "You're spiraling," I said. My hands were still on his chest.

Wow, his pecs were solid.

"Then let's lay down."

"No."

"Come on," he said slowly.

"You're looking for a distraction. You feel out-of-control, so you're trying to create another out-of-control situation so the rest of your life doesn't stand out so much in comparison. But you don't want this," I said, motioning back and forth between us. "You don't want me. You want to find your son, and I'm here to help."

He stared at me. At first, his eyes were on my mouth, and I regretted the plum lipstick I'd applied in the car. But as I spoke, I watched his eyes move from my lips to my eyes. I felt his energy shift.

"How?" he asked.

"Everybody else is looking at individual pieces of this whole thing, right? Madden is looking for Hans Braeburn's murderer. You're looking for Jameson. The Philadelphia police are looking for a serial killer."

"What are you looking for?" Dante asked. His eyes were on mine, boring deep into my brain, as if he stared hard enough he could see the answer to his question without me speaking.

"The thing that connects all of the above."

"What's that?"

I thought about everything I'd heard so far, the theories I'd floated to Madden, the details of the crimes in Philadelphia, and the reason I'd been at Braeburn Castle in the first place. "I think this might be about the jeans."

19

DOT. DOT. DOT. DOT

DANTE TURNED AWAY FROM ME AND MY ARMS FELL TO MY sides. "Think about it," I said. "Hans was the jeans specialist for the guild. I was going to be his replacement, and we were the two people who were drugged that night." I was talking to Dante's back, but I continued anyway. "The boys who were abducted in the Philadelphia area were all wearing jeans, and they were all found in their underwear." He still didn't turn around. "The guy I talked to that night, who I would bet my new Toyota Supra is Jameson, was in the study where all those jeans were. Two days later, the most valuable garment in the archives of the castle—a pair of jeans—is missing."

Dante turned around and looked at me. I jabbed my finger at the air. "Dot. Dot. Dot. Dot. They're all connected."

"Nobody at Braeburn Castle remembers seeing a red-headed guy but you. If I didn't know you, I'd think you made a mistake."

It was comforting, in a world where I spent large

amounts of time trying to convince people I was right, that someone trusted me because, despite my unbelievable claims, he knew my track record for figuring things out.

"I think your son is living there. Hiding, more likely. I think Hans was the one person who knew it, and he tolerated Jameson's presence." I remembered their altercation, the sound of a slap, and the red mark on Jameson's face. Dante was right; I didn't know Jameson. I didn't know what he was capable of, and I couldn't say for sure he hadn't been the one to murder Hans. "I think Jameson knows who killed Hans Braeburn," I finished. A delicately worded truth.

And then something kicked in. Some instinct to protect this boy who'd been raised by a single mother and knew his dad from time spent together on nights and weekends. This young man who'd gotten mixed up with an older crowd who fought, who'd come home beaten and bruised, who'd been told he was going to live with his dad for a while. He needed Dante as much as Dante needed him. He wouldn't have run away. This wasn't a case of a teenager giving life the middle finger.

"We have to get to the castle," I said.

Dante grabbed his motorcycle keys and headed toward the door. He put his hand on the knob, but something stopped him. He turned back and pocketed his keys. "You drive."

The ride was in silence. Dante wasn't prone to idle chatter, and the situation didn't warrant forced small talk. There was no point trying to find a covert parking space since I was driving a bright blue sports car, so I took the spot closest to the front door. It was propped open.

Marguerite was in the vestibule dusting a hutch filled with vintage beer steins.

"Hello, Samantha," she said. "Is this your husband?" She looked at Dante, and then back to me. Dante stepped closer and grabbed my hand.

"Um, yes," I said nervously. "This is Nick."

Marguerite smiled warmly. "Nice to meet you, Nick," she said.

I pointed down the hallway. "I came to organize the rest of the study. I abandoned the folding project mid-way."

"Go right ahead. I hate that room." She shuddered. "So dark and all those weird noises from the tree outside scraping against the window."

I led the way. From the outside, Braeburn Castle was huge, and I'd seen a relatively small portion of the interior. It would take days to go through the building looking for someone, and if that person didn't want to be found, it would be easy enough for them to move from place to place to protect their location. Even if Jameson were still here, if he didn't want to be found, he could easily fool us.

We reached the study. The room looked bigger now that the piles of jeans had been moved into storage. The air smelled faintly of lemons.

"Someone's been working in here," I said.

"Could be the maid."

"Only one way to find out. Wait here." I went back to the vestibule. "Marguerite," I said, "Did you clean in the study?"

"Yes," she said. "That black powder got onto everything so I went over it again."

"Has anyone else been in there?"

"Only Wilhelm."

For as creepy as the castle was, it was charming rooms were left open for the cat to come and go as he pleased. He seemed to be more in charge than anyone I'd met yet, including Hans himself.

"How long have you worked here?" I asked.

"Most of my life. Mr. Hans hired me when I was a teenager."

"Was he ever mean to you?"

"Mean? No. When I started working here, he told me what he wanted me to do, and I did it. One time I did straighten the study, and he was very mad. He told me that room contains his personal work papers and was not my responsibility. From then on, I left it alone."

"When was that?"

"Long time ago," she said. "Twenty years. We recently celebrated our anniversary."

"Hans threw you a party?"

"Not Hans. My family. My husband is the landscaper. This is where we met."

Marguerite finished dusting a heavy pewter beer stein and set it back in the hutch. She closed the doors and turned the key, leaving it inserted in the case. A fat black tassel hung from the key and gently rocked back and forth.

"Where do you keep the key?" I asked.

She laughed. "Right where it is," she said. "Mr. Hans used to keep the keys in a cabinet in the library, but he did not like to be interrupted when it was time for me to clean. He gave me a skeleton key and we set up a schedule for which wing to clean on each day."

I'd started questioning Marguerite to find out about the study, but now it was a different room that I remembered. "What about upstairs?" I asked. "The locked archives. Do you ever clean them?"

"Once a week," she said. "Even with air filters and temperature control, the rooms can get dusty."

"When did you clean them last?"

She thought for a moment. "Last week. I was due to clean them yesterday, but the police left such a mess I spent the morning laundering the jeans from the study."

I thanked her and headed back into the hallway. I tried to remember the day I'd been with Ahn in the archives. Had the door been unlocked? No. She'd already been inside. But did that mean the rooms were always unlocked? Did all members of the guild have a skeleton key? Did it give them access to places they might normally not go?

I couldn't shake the feeling that everything that had happened since I'd first entered the castle on the night of my interview was connected, yet I didn't know how.

I returned to the study. Dante wasn't there. Instead of heading off on a wild goose chase, I called him. Creepy castles had nothing on cell phone technology.

"Yo," he said.

"Where are you?"

"Out back. I couldn't see last night, I wanted to check the perimeter to see if anything looked suspicious."

"How'd you get past me? I was with Marguerite by the front door."

"There's a staff entrance in the kitchen."

"Okay. Meet me back in the study when you're done."

"Don't forget—if anyone asks, I'm your husband."

"We'll talk about that later." I hung up.

With the piles of pants now gone from the study, the room was easy to negotiate. I looked up at the bindings of the books on the shelf. They'd been recently dusted. The carpet had been vacuumed, and even the textured glass window behind the desk had been wiped free from fingerprint residue. I dragged my index finger across the surface of the desk. All traces of the mess left by the police were gone.

Like before, I sensed something off about this room. I walked across the carpet, around the desk, to the window. The textured glass distorted the outside world into giant blobs of green, brown, blue: grass, tree, sky. The castle sat on acres of lawn, ensuring privacy. A blurry dot of movement across the lawn caught my attention. It took a few seconds to realize it was a man cutting the grass.

Could I live in a castle? Hans had. For seventy-seven years. According to what Carl had uncovered in the *Ribbon Eagle* archives, Hans Braeburn had come to America in the mid-forties to escape being tried for war crimes and lived an unremarkable life until he died.

Did that make this a castle or a fortress?

The idea of living here suddenly felt like a self-imposed quarantine. How does one live an unremarkable life? How does one exist for seventy-seven years with the knowledge that they've committed atrocities of war? And how does one keep those secrets from the person they pledge to love for eternity?

Carl had told me Hans's wife died in the same fire that killed his parents. I wondered what her life had been like. If I'd been told to live here, I might have felt like a prisoner.

I moved from the window to the bookcase and scanned the book spines. At first glance, the titles appeared to run the gamut of classics: Dickens, Dumas, Nabokov, Shakespeare. But the shelf at the top of the bookcase was filled with leather-bound yearbooks. The years were out of order, which struck me as unusual in a house that otherwise seemed to place an unprecedented amount of importance on detail and organization.

I pushed a chair toward the bookcase, climbed up, and pulled the out-of-order books off the shelf. The years were displayed on the spine: '44, '54, '55, '66. I blew across the tops of the pages, but no cloud of dust appeared. Marguerite had done a thorough job.

I set the books on a lower shelf. Carefully, I climbed back down and then moved the stack of books from the shelf to the desk. I pulled the top one off the stack. It was from three years ago. As I reached the senior photos, I found a page where a picture had been removed. It seemed silly, to cut your picture from your yearbook, as if it was so embarrassing you wanted to destroy the evidence.

I set that yearbook aside and flipped open the next one. This one was from 1971. I chuckled at the styles worn by the students. I held the stack of pages in my left hand and let them fall in a cascade from the back. A book-mark marked a page toward the front that was also missing a photo. This time it was from the faculty section.

This no longer felt like someone who hadn't liked their yearbook photo.

I flipped through the first four yearbooks and found four missing pictures. It was easy to cross-reference the index to find the identity of missing students by finding the person before and after the cut-out photo, but the faculty photo took a bit more effort. I had no reason for the project save for curiosity and a growing sense of unease until I looked up the name of the student from the most recent yearbook. The name cross-referenced with the missing photo was Jameson's friend, Regan Weaver.

Before the thought was fully formed, I called Carl at the newspaper. "I need you to look something up."

"Call research. I'm on deadline."

"It could be a story," I said quickly. He didn't hang up. "I have a list of names and I need to know if they're connected."

Dante entered the study. I held my finger in front of my mouth to keep him quiet, then read off the names to Carl. They were all male and had come from a range of yearbooks spanning seventy-seven years.

I heard Carl's fingers tapping on his keyboard. He repeated the first two names, and after the third, said, "Kidd, if this is a joke, it's in poor taste."

"It's not a joke. Why? Who are they?"

"They're all murder victims." He gave me a moment to say something, but I was too stunned to speak. "What are you into now?"

20

THREE-QUARTERS OF A CENTURY

"Carl, I need to make another phone call."

"No can do, Kidd. *I'm* crime. You're fashion. You're not scooping me on a murder case."

"It's your story," I promised. "But I need to talk to a source." I hung up before he said another word.

I got down from the chair and pushed it behind the desk. "What did you find?" Dante asked.

I gestured to the yearbooks on the desk. "Each one is missing a photo. Some students, some faculty. One of them is Jameson's friend Regan."

"From what Linda told me, Regan wasn't a friend. He's the guy who got Jameson into trouble."

"According to Carl, with the exception of Regan, these guys were all murdered." I tapped the top of the yearbook stack. "The first murder was in 1944, and the most recent was a few years ago. Three-quarters of a century." A sickening thought came into my mind. "I don't think Hans has been living an unremarkable life." And whether due to the strong suspicion of what Hans had done or my first bout of morning sickness, I bent over and threw up in the trash.

FORTY-FIVE MINUTES LATER, Detective Madden and his team were back at the castle. I called him after getting sick, and he confirmed that the names from the yearbooks were murder victims. Two of them, from 1955 and 1966, had died similarly, but their deaths hadn't been connected to the jean jackings in Philadelphia until now.

After blowing his mind with my discovery in the yearbooks, Madden told me to wait for him to arrive. Dante kept himself out of the investigation by leaving on foot. Since a lack of vehicle would have raised questions about how I'd gotten there, I couldn't offer him the use of my car.

The study had been dusted for fingerprints once, and the thorough cleaning job had eradicated anything the police might have missed. Madden seemed undaunted by the newly organized room. He led me to the clubroom while two uniformed officers collected the evidence in the study. We sat in leather wingback chairs, and I gave him my narrative account of finding the yearbooks.

"They were out of order," I said. "The dates on the spines weren't chronological. That's what caught my eye. The other times I was in the study I was focused on all the jeans in there, but today, I looked at the books. I found the missing photos, and when I called my contact at the paper to see if there was anything unusual about the names, he told me all but one were murder victims."

"Did he tell you anything else?"

"I'm pretty sure at that point, I knew more than him."

"Did you tell *him* anything else?"

"No. I called you. How does this relate to the boys who were abducted in Philadelphia? Are these men—were these men—found in their underwear too?"

"We don't know. Cell phone and traffic camera technology don't date back to the earliest of those crimes. There's a fifty-year gap between the last two yearbooks—"

"But the presence of that yearbook says these crimes were done by the same person. You're investigating that angle, right?"

"We're not ruling anything out."

"I don't want to sound like I'm trying to do your job, but don't the missing photos indicate premeditation? Like the victims were chosen ahead of time?"

"We don't know if the photos were cut out before or after the murders."

That slowed my gyrating mind. "If they were cut out after the murders, then that would mean..." My voice trailed off. I tipped my head away from Madden and tried to conjure up a plausible scenario for that. "The killer commits a murder of a somewhat random nature, and then takes the victim's jeans, and then goes out and finds a yearbook with the victim's picture in it and cuts it out? That seems more than crazy."

"It does."

One of the uniformed officers who'd arrived with Madden stood in the doorway. "We found something else," he said.

Madden stood, and I followed. The officers led us back to the study. A black and white employee directory from an international bank sat on top of the desk. Madden glanced at the officer, who nodded, and then he flipped it open. The front page showed the president, vice president, and two international client officers. The photo of the officer in the lower left-hand corner was missing, and I was too far away to read the caption.

"Where did you find this?" Madden asked.

The officer pointed to the top shelf.

"Was the international client officer another victim?" I asked,

Madden bent over the page and read the caption, and then stood up. "He's a she. The international client officer was named Cecile Sézane."

"Cecile is a member of the guild," I said. I pulled my phone out of my back pocket and did an internet search. "This is her." I held my phone up for Madden and the officers to see.

"Do you have her contact information?"

"No, but I know someone who does."

I tapped the favorites on my phone and called Eddie. I hadn't thought much about how many men there were in my life, and how few women. Being invited to join the guild had felt like an endorsement of my fashion side, an acknowledgment of my connection to the world of clothes and style, and that had always felt like a feminine pursuit. Cecile, Lucy, and Ahn had helped shape that perception, but aside from them, I'd been surrounded by men. I really did need some positive female influences.

"Dude," Eddie answered.

"Hi. Are you busy?"

"I'm painting accessories into a reproduction mural of Michelangelo's Creation of Man. Why?"

I was temporarily speechless. Some things shock even me.

"Do you have Cecile Sézane's phone number? From the guild. I need to talk to her."

"She's out of the country," Eddie said.

"How could you possibly know that off the top of your head?"

"Email from the guild. They sent out a press release about Hans. With him gone, she's the acting president. She sent a separate note stating that the guild will host a benefit in his honor when she returns from France next week."

"Cecile's in France?" I glanced at Madden to see if he was listening in. He was. "Paris?"

"Vichy."

"What's in Vichy?"

"Cecile's family. Something unexpected came up. I don't think she planned it."

Riiiiiight. A family emergency takes her out of the country in the wake of Hans's murder. It seemed convenient at best, but my mind wasn't hardwired to accept convenient excuses.

Cecile and Hans had known each other a long time, and the timing of her leaving the country felt suspicious. *What if...*

As I stared at the space where her photo should have been, I felt chills to my core. There were two plausible possibilities, and neither was good.

Cecile didn't seem like a murderer, but that was because I didn't believe murderers could be in their late seventies and wear couture. If she harbored a grudge against him for decades, would she eventually snap?

The other alternative was worse. The email Eddie received about a guild emergency could have been faked. Someone had killed Hans, and I'd believed it was justice over past crimes. But if Hans's murder was connected to the guild, then Cecile could have been a target too.

I'd told Dante the dots were connected, but maybe those dots were a distraction to keep a member from wearing prison stripes.

21

LAUGHABLE

I SAID GOODBYE TO EDDIE. HE WAS USED TO ABRUPT endings to our calls, though I suspected he'd lecture me on generally accepted phone etiquette the next time we spoke.

I wasn't ready to leave the castle, but Detective Madden didn't allow me to stick around. "It's after three. I can't reseal the crime scene, but until I get a few answers, I'd like to preserve whatever evidence I can. That means I can't let you stay."

"Sure," I said. "Let me get my handbag."

Madden moved his arm from behind him and held out my bag. Reluctantly, I took it. It wasn't like I knew what I wanted to check out on one last trip to the study, but his considerate gesture kept me from having an excuse to go back to the scene of the crime.

Maybe that was the point?

I drove away first. My mind was buzzing with information, but aside from a potentially new direction, I didn't know what any of it meant. The truth was, I knew nothing about the people in the organization I'd been invited to pledge and nothing about the garment I'd been auditioning to represent. It wasn't until the night of my interview that I learned I was being groomed as their jeans expert.

Jeans. Of all the classic designs through history, they gave me *jeans.*

It was laughable. I could identify the factory used for the silk braid on a Chanel jacket or the construction site of a pair of Belgian loafers. I was one of a dozen people who knew directions to the factory in Parabiago, Italy that produced eighty pairs of Manolo Blahniks a day. But jeans were one of those garments that had become a classic by default. Levi Strauss hadn't opened an atelier on the Rue de Cambon like Coco Chanel had in 1910 or participated in the infamous Battle of Versailles in 1973. Denim had been around since 17th century France. A tailor knew Strauss made work pants and brought him the idea for a copper rivet to reinforce stress points. Together, they got a patent, used the rivets in their new pants, and improved upon workwear for men during the California gold rush.

At least I remembered something from Denim 101.

Jeans hadn't been appropriated by the fashion world until the eighties when Calvin Klein, Jordache, and Gloria Vanderbilt owned the category, followed by colorful acid-washed styles, but by the nineties, grunge was in full swing. Instead of fancy back-pocket stitching and designer labels, fashion could be had with a couple of bucks and a trip to Goodwill. It took a decade for designer jeans to come back in full force, and even that was more about style and label than fabric and construction. Some of those jeans were so loaded with stretch, you could buy a pair two sizes too small and still get them zipped.

A post-college life of retail buying allowed me to treat every day like a fashion show, and the singular pair of jeans I'd bought were ones I'd gotten with my employee discount. But some rules governed our dress code and one included no jeans while traveling on the company dime. I'd gotten used to thinking jeans were anti-fashion and had only started wearing them regularly since moving back to Ribbon. (Amateur sleuthing is far more productive when you're not worried about messing up your clothes.)

I never gave much thought to Levi's before now. Lee was the brand worn by James Dean in *Rebel Without a Cause*, but the company didn't associate themselves with the actor the way Tiffany's had associated with Audrey Hepburn. And Wranglers had been linked with western wear. When it came to the history of jeans as a fashion classic, I was in over my head.

I drove home. Logan met me by the front door. I scooped him up and scratched his ears. "How's my little soldier?" I asked. He gave me a funny look. "Sorry. How's my little prince?"

He closed his eyes halfway and purred.

I carried him upstairs and set him on a pile of T-shirts. He meowed, and then moved to a stack of plaid skirts, stuck one foot in the air, and started cleaning himself. I gave him his privacy (though he clearly didn't need it) and sat down at Nick's computer to do a deep dive into denim.

BY THE TIME Nick came home hours later, I was, once again surrounded by clothes. Unfortunately for the condition of our house, this time the clothes were in the bedroom. And unfortunately for Nick, the clothes were his.

As Nick studied the piles on the floor, I studied him. Strands of shiny silver had shown up in his dark, curly hair, and the crinkles by his eyes had become more permanent even when he wasn't smiling. His eyes were set off by shadows underneath. He wore a lavender polo shirt with jeans and sneakers, today a pair of ecru leather and suede samples that had been delivered from a shoe-making factory in Maine. I admired his desire to bring his production stateside, but it had been a series of one step forward, two steps back. Considering 99 percent of all shoes sold in the USA were made in other countries, watching Nick trying to achieve his goal was a bit like watching Sisyphus push a boulder up a mountain.

He kissed me hello, but his eyes didn't leave the pile on the floor. "I know I haven't read Marie Kondo's book yet but aren't you supposed to worry about *your* clothes? I thought my stuff was supposed to spark joy for *me.*"

"This isn't about joy sparking," I said. I held a pair of faded jeans by the bottom and turned the opening inside out. "You have seventeen pairs of selvedge jeans." As evidence, I ran my fingers over the inside seam where the factory-finished fabric edge was visible. It was a mark of quality and craftsmanship ever since companies had abandoned the practice in favor of faster production.

"And?"

"Do you even know what selvedge means?"

"Of course, I know what it means. I bought them, didn't I?"

"Seventeen pairs is a lot."

"Have you looked in the spare bedroom lately?"

"And this 'XX' on the leather tag on your 501s," I said, holding up a dark pair. "That indicates shrink-to-fit. You're supposed to sit in the bathtub in these. I never saw you do that. Did you do that? Isn't shrink-to-fit risky? What if your size changes? What if you gain weight?" I glanced at Nick's body. "We've been married for over a year. Why haven't you gained weight?"

He took the jeans from me and laid them on the bed. "One might make the argument that shrink-to-fit is the couture of denim."

I picked up another pair. "This pair weighs a ton. How do you wear these?" I stretched the jeans taut and did a couple of bicep curls, then tried to stand them upright. (It almost worked.)

"Those are 20 oz denim. I bought them on a whim."

"A whim? I didn't know you shopped on whims." I felt closer to Nick than usual. "I shop on whims all the time. You're just like me!"

His eyes widened. I threw my arms around his torso and he tentatively returned the embrace and patted my back.

"What's this about, Kidd?"

I stepped back. "I came home and started researching jeans. For the guild, you know? And then I wanted to see some examples, so I looked at the ones I swiped from my dad, but that wasn't enough to learn anything, so I came in here to check your closet. I had no idea you had so many jeans."

He eyed the pile on the floor. "Where did these come from?"

"The closet. I'll hang them back up when I'm done, but Marie says they should be folded."

Nick turned around and went to his dresser. He pulled out the bottom drawer. Inside were small sausages of denim lined up next to each other.

"What are they?"

"More. From Japan. I went nuts when I was in Tokyo last year."

I followed him across the room and pulled a pair out. The denim was softer than any of the jeans I'd found hanging in his closet. The tag on the back was Vachetta leather like on the Levi's, but the picture featured two samurais facing off with swords. The brand was Samurai Genuine Jeans made in Osaka, Japan.

"You wear jeans a lot now, don't you?" I asked.

"Every day."

"You used to wear suits."

"Sometimes, yes. For market appointments and business meetings. But when I'm not meeting with buyers, I spend 90% of my time in a shoe factory."

"Yes, but you don't work on the line," I said. He raised his eyebrow. "You know what I mean."

He took my hand and pulled me to the bed. We sat facing each other. "How do you not know about the history of denim?"

Considering my excuse for failing Denim 101 included a college boyfriend, I chose not to answer Nick's question.

He gestured toward the pile on the floor. "Jeans are more than work pants. They're classic American fashion." He bent down and picked up a pair of Levi's. "This pair is a reissue. A replica of the Levi's that were made in 1954."

"When they first used a zipper."

"You *do* know something about jeans."

"I've been binging content for the past five hours."

I took the jeans from his hand. They were labeled 501Z. The website said the zipper was added when the company wanted to gain a new audience on the East Coast who wasn't familiar with button fly work pants.

"Do you have any other reissues?"

He squatted next to the pile and flipped through the mess, pulling out a somewhat odd-looking pair that had a tab across the back yoke and were missing a back pocket.

"1873 reissue. Modeled after the first 501s."

I took the jeans and held them up. They looked less like a classic five-pocket jean, the model for all modern denim these days, and more like a one-off, maybe something Isaac Mizrahi would have included in the same collection where he debuted paper-bag-waist pants. "I've never seen you wear these."

He shrugged. "They don't fit anymore, but I can't bring myself to throw them out."

"Can I try them on?"

"Sure."

One of the benefits of marriage is the familiarity factor. Nick had watched me change clothes thousands of times in our still-relatively-new marriage thanks to my outfit indecision, so stripping down to my undies in front of him now was no big deal. I took off my dad's now-filthy white jeans and then pulled on Nick's. They eased over my hips, were a little snug in the inner thigh area, but overall, they fit. I stepped over the pile on the floor and turned my butt toward the floor-length mirror to see the back.

"They look great on you," Nick said. His voice was husky. "You should wear them."

"They look a little masculine."

"Not on you they don't." He spun me around and kissed me, and in a few minutes, the jeans were back on the floor.

When we finished our midday dalliance, I left Nick with the mess I'd made of his closet and returned to the spare bedroom. I sorted through my original pile of discards. The other pair of my dad's old jeans were still on it. Armed with the curiosity that comes from a little bit of knowledge, I examined them. They had a button fly, a 501 patch, and a red tab that said LEVI'S in uppercase. I carried them to Nick.

"What can you tell me about these?"

He took the jeans and inspected them. "Pre-1980, so they're not a reissue. The leg is slim. I'd guess they're mid-sixties."

"You can tell all that from a pair of jeans?"

"The 'E' in 'LEVI'S' is in caps. They didn't switch to the lowercase 'e' until 1971. The leg got slimmer in the sixties, too." He kissed the tip of my nose. "You'll be able to see it too once you know what to look for."

It had been a long time since I indulged in the history of fashion. My life, since moving back to Ribbon, had been more about trying to find my footing while occasionally getting mixed up in local crime-solving.

It felt good to shift my attention to something

completely new, to learn about a corner of fashion history I'd never indulged in before, but some piece of information tickled my brain like an itch I couldn't scratch.

I took the jeans from Nick and went to leave, but then turned back. "How many reissues did Levi's do?"

"I don't know off the top of my head, but it shouldn't be hard to find out. There's the '44, the '54, the '55, and the '66. What's wrong? Why are you looking at me like that?"

I felt my response to Nick's information before the realization crystallized in my mind.

The blood drained from my face, and the same chill I'd felt at the castle returned. I recognized those years. I knew them before Nick said them. I'd seen those same numbers last night.

"Those were the years on the yearbooks in the study."

That was it. That was what had been bothering me. The years of the reissues perfectly matched up with the years each of the murders had taken place.

SOMEWHAT FREE FROM SUSPICION

"I HAVE TO TALK TO DETECTIVE MADDEN," I SAID.

Nick thrust his phone at me. Madden's contact information was cued up. I tapped the number and despite the late hour, the detective answered.

"The dates on the yearbooks line up with the years Levi's made changes to their 501 patterns."

"Who is this?"

"Samantha Kidd," I said. "I borrowed Nick's phone," I added.

"What's this about?"

"The yearbooks we found in the study. I think it has something to do with him identifying his victims."

"Who?"

"Hans Braeburn. He killed them. He's the one who murdered those men and took their jeans. It fits. He's a denim expert, and he was obsessed. He must have stalked them for their jeans and then—"

"Samantha." Madden's voice came out calmly, but if I were the overly sensitive type, I might say it leaned toward judgmental. "We're taking the evidence found today into advisement while continuing to look for Mr. Braeburn's murderer."

"But this connects back to that. It's motive. Someone found out what Hans did. They killed him over it. Maybe it was Cecile. She was at the castle the night he was murdered, and we already connected her to the books in the study. Maybe she cut out her picture to throw off suspicion. Did you talk to her? Is she still in France? Did she tell you anything about what she does for the bank or her ties to Hans or the yearbooks?"

"The police department appreciates your cooperation, but you know I can't talk to you about a person of interest. It would compromise the investigation."

"So, she's a person of interest," I said, reading between the lines.

"Everyone who was at the castle the night Mr. Braeburn was murdered is a person of interest," Madden said.

"What about me?"

"You're somewhat free from suspicion."

I'd come up against the lines between friendship and policework many times before, but that didn't make me like them any more now. Madden was a friend, and I treated him as such. It wasn't like the old days when Detective Loncar was the one in charge. It was easier to ignore the police when *I'd* been a person of interest in a case, but this time, I was a witness.

"Good. Okay." I changed the subject. "What about Dante's son? Are there any leads on Jameson? Or Regan, the guy in the photo with him. Is he still missing too?"

Madden didn't answer right away. In a flash, I understood his conflict of interest. Me placing Jameson at the scene of the murder made him more than a missing four-teen-year-old boy. It made him a person of interest too. A wrong step in one direction could cost Madden his job. A wrong step in the other could cost him a relationship.

"You know, I may have been mistaken when I said I saw Jameson at the castle," I said slowly. "I didn't get a good look at that guy. It was dark, and there were all those piles of jeans, and you already know I have an active imagination…"

"Samantha," Madden said. "I appreciate what you're trying to do."

"Is it working?"

"Thank you for the tip. I'll follow up on your information." He hung up.

Police work, I've learned, is by the book in more ways than one. If someone gives the police a tip concerning an open case, they *must* follow up on it. Not following up would show negligence, and negligence opens the police up to criticism.

Fortunately, amateur sleuthing was only bound by the limits of my determination and the number of people in my life who enable my unwise choices.

"Kidd, you have that look on your face," Nick said. "What are you about to do?"

"Me? Nothing. I'm—I—Eddie. I'm going to call Eddie."

Nick narrowed his eyes as if parsing what it was I had planned, but I left before his line of questioning really got underway.

THE NEXT DAY, I met Eddie for lunch. When I called him last night, he'd gotten out of an Epson salt bath and was in no shape to get redressed and meet to discuss the case. He promised to hear out everything I had to say if I gave him a solid eight hours to sleep. Since Eddie rarely required a full night of sleep, it was the least I could do.

We agreed to meet at a Mexican restaurant that used to be our favorite diner. It had been better as a diner than a Mexican joint, but the positive energy of the place kept it in my top ten spots to eat, which was more than I could say for the breakfast spot that used to be a seafood restaurant. Ribbon was slowly discarding the shell of its past and becoming something new. Kind of like a cicada.

Today I dressed in Nick's 1873 Levi's reissue, belted tightly with a heavy brown leather belt to keep them sitting at my waist, a camel-colored cowl-neck sweater, and a matching camelhair blazer. The sleeves on the sweater were extra-long and hung out well past the cuffs of the blazer, covering my knuckles. I pushed both up so I could eat, and the fabric bunched at my elbows, making it difficult to bend my arms. Sometimes fashion requires sacrifice.

Eddie was a big fan of message tees and today he wore one that said, JUST SAY NO TO YES MEN. His bleached blond hair was Einstein-chic. It stuck out in every direction, as if he'd licked his finger and stuck it into an electrical socket.

I caught Eddie up on the Hans/Jameson/Regan/Madden/Dante situation, and since Eddie was one of my enabling forces, the conversation flowed easily. "I'm the one who insisted the guy I saw was Jameson, and now it looks like Jameson might have killed Hans. It looks like

Hans killed a whole bunch of people first, so whoever killed him might have been going for revenge."

Eddie put a tortilla on his plate and filled it with sizzling chicken and beef. "You said the yearbooks dated back to 1944?"

"Yep. Hans was ninety-five years old. He moved here in forty-four. Think about it. Here's this Nazi who comes to the states to live. His family died in a fire, and he's been alone in there ever since. Who knows what goes on in that building?"

Eddie shrugged. "The Fahrenheit Guild met there regularly and I never noticed anything out of sorts."

"That's it. The guild was so secret I never even heard of it. Doesn't that seem odd? I grew up in Ribbon like you. I majored in fashion at a local college, and I worked in the industry my whole life."

"You left," he said with a mouth full of fajita. He swallowed. "I learned about the guild through Tradava. I never told you about them because you used to keep threatening to move back to New York and the guild is interested in residents who have no intention of leaving the area."

"When did you nominate me?"

"After that case with the pretzel heiress." He grinned. "You get free cases of pretzels sent to your house every month. No way are you going to move now."

"You never told me who nominated you."

"Buck Hollinger. Before you moved back to Ribbon, Tradava did a western event. I made a fake Nudie suit for the store window—"

"You put a Nudie on display at Tradava?" I had to laugh. Nudie Cohn was to country singers what Bob Mackie was to Cher. "Only a true artiste would hear 'western event' and think 'Nudie suit.'" I snapped a corn chip in half. "This is why we're friends."

"The store's customer base wasn't as open-minded as you are. Sales dropped by double digits. Two days after the event kicked off, the store manager had me change my Nudie mannequin into Wranglers and a plaid shirt." He sat back, disgusted by the lack of vision.

"What happened to your knockoff?"

"Buck saw it before I tore it down. He's an expert on Nudie Cohn. We kept in touch. When I turned forty last year, the invitation showed up."

"Did you have to go through a vetting process like mine?"

He shook his head. "Accessories aren't the same as garments. We don't have voting privileges, and no more than ten percent of the budget goes toward our acquisitions."

"Then what do you get?"

"Meeting attendance, networking opportunities," he rolled his eyes, "and access to the archives."

"You mean you get to visit your Vans whenever you want? Considering you have a closet filled with them, that's hardly a perk."

"Not the archives for my item, but *all* the archives. I've borrowed garments for store display more than once."

"The guild lets you take things out of the castle?"

"If the garment's representative agrees," Eddie said. He layered chicken and beef from the fajita tray into a second tortilla and tried to wrap it, then removed two strips of beef to make it a more reasonable size. "Don't judge."

"How could I possibly judge you?" I asked. "You've seen how I eat."

"Speaking of which, why did you order a salad?"

Nick and I had agreed to keep our news to ourselves until tests from the OB-GYN made it official, but that didn't stop me from changing some habits. "I'm trying to improve my diet." I jabbed my fork into the bowl a few times, coming up with a slice of avocado and a sliver of apple. "Back to the guild. If I wanted to borrow a garment, what's the procedure?"

"You're not a member."

"I'm *almost* a member." I set down my fork. "Fine. I'm not a member, but you are. If *you* wanted to borrow a garment, what do you have to do?"

"Get written permission from the representative, which goes into a secure file, and then you both sign off on a logbook that's kept in the archive room."

"If a garment is missing, there would be a paper trail of who accessed it."

"Technically, yes, but guild garments don't go missing. Some of those samples are fragile and irreplaceable. It's rare for someone to check one out."

"But you did."

"That's right. And I had the full cooperation of a guild member."

"A guild member who happened to be present the night of a recent murder," I said. "How well do you know Buck? He went out on a limb to get you into the guild just this year. Have you ever wondered why? Are you friends? Do you see each other socially?" I stopped to consider other options. "Maybe he *likes you* likes you. Did he ever hit on you?"

Eddie checked his watch and then glared at me. "How long is this going to go on? Because I've learned not to encourage you when you have bouts of temporary insanity."

I leaned forward. "He was in the room when I was drugged, he was still at the castle when I found Hans's body. He was drinking in the bar with Lucy."

"Nothing suspicious about that," he said. "They're drinking buddies. They get drunk together after every guild meeting."

Which meant if one of them killed Hans, they'd already set the stage to have an alibi.

23

DARK CORNERS

I TEMPORARILY FORGOT ABOUT THE MISSING JEANS. "CAN you get me a meeting with Buck?" I asked.

"'A meeting'?" Eddie asked. "Who do you think he is, Tony Soprano? Buck's a hipster with a lot of money. That makes him fun to be around, but not particularly deep. If you ask him about that night, he'll probably tell you about the bourbon they lifted from the bar."

"Perfect," I said. "I've been thinking of buying Nick a bottle of Bourbon for Christmas. This way I'll know I consulted an expert." I reached across the table and slid Eddie's fajita plate away from him. "Call him now before I cut off your lunch."

AFTER LOSING A COIN TOSS, Eddie left his VW Bug at the restaurant, and I drove us to Buck's apartment. I was initially surprised to learn that a fourth-generation hipster lived in a rental property, until Eddie told me

Buck bought the building as an investment and kept the top floor for himself.

When we reached Buck's floor, he greeted us at the elevator. I guess owning the building gets you a phone call when visitors arrive.

"Eddie," Buck said. He hugged Eddie (that was unexpected) and then nodded at me. "Samantha Kidd, right?" he asked. He pointed back and forth between us. "How do you two cats know each other?"

"Work," I said while Eddie said, "High school." Buck nodded as if the answer didn't matter to him and then led us inside. We reached a wide-open living room filled with a black leather sectional and an unfair amount of Eames chairs.

"What brings you to mi casa?" he asked. While Eddie and I took seats on the sofa, Buck poured himself a drink from a fully-stocked bar cart. He pointed to the glasses and then to us, and both of us shook our heads. Eddie shot me a look that said, "I got you in the door, now it's up to you," or maybe it said, "tell him why you're here and I'll sit back and laugh." I thought highly of Eddie, so I dismissed both interpretations and assumed he'd sat on a broken spring.

I tossed out the requisite compliment of Buck's living space while he switched on ambient lighting. When we entered, I'd noticed framed black and white photographs on his walls, but it wasn't until now that I saw the subject matter. I inhaled sharply, and Buck cracked a smile.

"They're vintage crime scene photos," he said. "Usually takes visitors a moment to react."

"You collect them?" I asked.

"I do. There's an honesty to them that you don't get in

most art." He lingered by a photo that showed a lifeless body on a Persian carpet. "These photos document what was probably the most exciting moment of the victim's life."

"No," I said without thinking.

He turned to face me. "What could be more exciting than knowing you're about to die?" The question hung in the air, and then he smiled. "They're a little dark for most people but I like the darkness. If you want, we can sit in the other living room."

"This is fine," I said while Eddie was in the process of standing. He glared at me and sat back down.

I chewed my lip and considered what I wanted to know. Buck had the harmless, too-cool-for-school air of someone who'd always been the most popular person in the room, and I wondered if that popularity was tied to his checkbook.

"I'm here about the guild," I said. "Things didn't go as planned on the night of my interview and I still have questions."

Buck glanced at Eddie, and then back at me. "Did you tell her the guild is like Fight Club?"

Eddie looked uncomfortable. "I didn't say anything—"

Buck slapped Eddie playfully. "Just kidding, man! It's cool." He came around to the front of the sofa and sat between me and Eddie. He looked over each shoulder as if checking for eavesdroppers. "I've never been one for rules. What do you want to know?"

Aside from the creepy crime scene photos, the décor was sleek and modern. Black leather was countered with tweed pillows. The floors were hardwood sanded to expose the grain. Faded vintage Mexican serapes were draped over a table that sat under a mounted cow skull. There was a studied style to the mix: world traveler meets bachelor. The result was pleasantly eclectic and decidedly male.

Money meant security for me. For Buck, it meant something else. Safe passage to the dark corners of life. I'd been in some dark corners too, but not because I sought them out.

Since buying my sports car, I'd had enough intersection encounters with men to see how they communicated when they wanted to know something. No wasted words. Ask and learn. It was a different form of aggression than I'd known, direct and to the point. I questioned how much time I'd wasted on pleasantries designed to ease people into a conversation, and I tested my theory with Buck.

"What can you tell me about Hans?" I asked. The question felt too direct, and I almost apologized for my bluntness when he answered.

"You met the man. What's your take on him?"

"When I look at Hans, I saw a crotchety old man who lives in a castle," I said. "He appeared to have no patience with outsiders."

"You're not wrong. When I first hooked up with the guild, I thought the same thing."

I leaned forward. "There has to be more than that. He was a German immigrant who started a secret fashion society. Doesn't that interest you? How a World War II soldier who fought for the bad guys came to start the Fahrenheit Guild in Ribbon, Pennsylvania?"

"You don't know the story?" Buck asked. I shook my head.

"Do you?" he asked Eddie, who shook his head too.

"Look up the name 'Braeburn' some time. Know what you'll find?" He paused long enough to indicate he hadn't expected an answer. "Old English, not German. Hans has ties to World War II because he *chose* the Nazi party. He helped run the *Deutsches Modeamt*—the Nazi Party's attempt to bring fascism to fashion. His parents got him out of Germany but he tried to bring the messaging here. A lot of soldiers who fought for Germany claimed they were following orders, but not Hans. He believed in the cause." He shook his head in disgust.

Everything Buck told me lined up with what Carl had dug up at the paper, but that did little to make it less troubling. I'd spent my whole life seeing fashion as an extension of identity, a way to show the world how you feel on the inside. And here was a man who saw the same thing, but what was on the inside was hatred.

"You heard about the fire, right?" Buck continued. "Killed every member of Hans's family. His wife was four months pregnant. A lot of people believed that fire was meant for him."

"That might incentivize a man to act out of hate," I said.

"Hans's whole life had been based on hate, and look what it got him. After that, he became a recluse. Hired staff and didn't leave. Nobody saw him for a decade. People forgot about the man in the castle. It's one of the reasons the guild membership is so secret. Hans established the organization, but he only allowed access to members approved through the vetting process."

"The same process I was about to go through."

"You were different. Cecile made a motion that we fill

Hans's position while he was still alive. He fought her but lost. I asked Eddie if he knew anybody who'd fit the bill, and he gave me your name."

I glanced at Eddie, who nodded. He didn't seem as proud of the suggestion now as he'd been when I first found out.

Something about Buck didn't fit in with the world of secret fashion societies, but I couldn't put my finger on what. He had the look. He had the money. He had the wherewithal, sure, but he lacked the interest in clothes, and that was at the core of the Fahrenheit Guild. From everything I'd been told, the first requirement of joining was a passion for the history of fashion. Members were recruited to memorize styles that would live on through members. Buck didn't seem passionate about the group, the fashion, or any of it.

"What was your point of entry?" I asked.

"A childhood friend. We met at summer camp when we were kids and stayed in touch. He was moving out of the country, and the guild bylaws provide a ten-day window for a member to select their replacement. He asked if I wanted his spot."

"Then you inherited the Nudie Suit," I said. "Do you even care about fashion history? Or is this a way to diversify your portfolio?"

"Dude," Eddie said.

"It's okay," Buck said to Eddie, though he didn't take his eyes off me "Yes, I donate money to the guild. Yes, I receive tax benefits for it. Yes, I was probably a good choice because of my bank account." He leaned back against the sofa and stretched his arms along the back, taking up more space than either Eddie or I and displaying an uncomfortable amount of confidence. "From what I understand, you recently came into some money yourself. Made life easier, didn't it?"

I couldn't disagree. When I gave up my New York life and moved back to Ribbon, I struggled financially. Job after job dissolved under my feet and almost cost me my relationship with Nick. A windfall from an anonymous donor who appreciated the role I played in the takedown of some corrupt businesspeople had changed my bank account overnight. It was how I was able to live life on the paltry salary of an occasional style column reporter and afford to galivant around Ribbon by day instead of punching a time clock.

(I know *you* know the time clock didn't stop me from gallivanting around Ribbon before the windfall, but let's say I'm less guilty about the gallivanting now that I mostly work for myself.)

Buck continued. "Money makes some things better, makes some things worse. Most of the time, I feel like I'm flatlining. No ups and downs. That's why I seek out the dark corners. Life doesn't come with defibrillators. Sometimes you've got to shock yourself to wake up."

"You mean jumping out of airplanes and rafting down the river?"

"There are different ways to find thrills. Nobody tells you the shocks are what makes life interesting. There's beauty in death. There's splendor in suffering." He reached out and traced his index finger across the image of a crime scene photo that was sitting on a table behind the sofa.

My stomach flipped. I glanced at Eddie to see if his

reaction was like mine. His eyes were wide, and he appeared to have scooted a few inches away from Buck.

I thought back to the night of the murder. Buck had been at the castle like Lucy, and Ahn, and Cecile, and Marguerite. Which one of them was responsible for killing Hans? Was the same man who represented the historical value of the suits made famous by country singers capable of taking Hans's life for the experience of watching a man die?

Nothing about this case made sense. Nothing. The clues and the evidence were still as random as cards dealt for a board game. Every one of the suspects appeared to dislike the victim. Every one of the suspects had a chance to kill him. And every one of the suspects acted like Hans's death was no big deal.

Whatever questions I'd hoped to answer from visiting with Buck had triggered a hundred more. Worse, the longer Eddie and I sat in Buck's living room, the more I wanted to leave. This wasn't my lifestyle, and all the money in the world wouldn't make me seek out dark corners—though to be fair, they seemed to find me anyway. If Buck needed a way to increase his heartbeat, maybe he should walk a mile in my shoes.

There was one question I hadn't asked and as much as I wanted to get out of there, I knew if I didn't ask it, I'd regret it forever.

"There's something I keep wondering about that night," I said. "There were six glasses set up in the board room. The water I drank was spiked. Hans's too. I know you drank rye from your flask, but if the water in the pitcher was spiked, then isn't it curious that Cecile, Lucy, and Ahn all knew not to drink it?"

Buck leaned forward and pulled a hand-rolled cigarette from a small silver box on his coffee table. He licked the end and then put it between his lips but didn't reach for a lighter. "That sounds like an accusation," he said.

"Of whom?" I asked, mostly because I wanted to hear who he'd finger of the crime.

"Of the one person you know didn't drink the water," he said. He pulled a metal lighter out of his shirt pocket and flicked it open, then lit the cigarette. "Be careful who you poke, Samantha. The others might not be as amused by you as I am."

I stood from the sofa and backed away from him. I tripped over Eddie's feet and fell to the sofa into Eddie's lap. I scrambled to my feet and put more distance between us.

We left. Neither one of us spoke until we were a few miles away. "That was weird, right?" I asked. "All that talk about dark corners and the splendor in suffering?"

"Dude, I don't know what to make of that conversation."

"He could have done it," I said. "Any of them could have done it. None of them cares that Hans is dead."

"Do you?"

I shrugged. "I know I should. Someone committed murder and they might get away with it. I care about justice. I always have. But this time..."

Eddie shifted in his seat. I felt his eyes on me even though mine were on the road. I glanced to my right to confirm my suspicion. "Why are you doing this?" he asked.

"I'm not the only person who shouldn't have been at

the castle the night Hans was murdered. Dante's son was there too. And because of me, he's in danger."

"You don't know that."

"I'm the one who placed him at the scene of the crime. I don't know him, I don't know what he's capable of, but my gut says he didn't do it. I know that's not enough. I know there's every possibility that he did. But I can't shake one thing."

"What's that?"

"If he wasn't there to kill Hans, then why was he there? Does he know something that's keeping him in hiding?"

"Like what?"

I shook my head. "What would have brought a teen from Philadelphia to a castle in the middle of Ribbon? How do those two things connect?"

"The answer is probably at the castle," Eddie said.

Eddie was, historically, the easiest of my friends to convince of my plans, not because he didn't know better, but because the decade he'd spent in Ribbon when I was in New York had lacked the excitement he discovered when I moved back. I relied on that now.

"You have access to the archives, right?" I asked him. "You can get in. You have a skeleton key."

Eddie held up his giant wad of keys. I'd often wondered why he carried so many but assumed it had to do with his job at the department store where he worked. Now he was self-employed, but the size of his keyring appeared to have grown. He singled out one iron key and pinched it between his thumb and index finger while the rest of the keys dangled.

"Are you up for an unscheduled field trip?"

24

COMMUNITY THEATER SKETCH

IT WAS A PARTY OF THREE, NOT TWO, THAT ARRIVED AT Braeburn Castle. We'd made a stop-off for Dante. It wasn't that we needed him per se, but anything that happened at the castle concerned Jameson, and keeping Dante in the loop kept him from spiraling out of control. Besides, if we planned to skulk about the archives, it didn't hurt to have someone distracting the staff. I parked out front, and Dante led the way.

"Eddie knows we're married, right?" he asked me.

"What?" Eddie asked.

I shot Dante a look of warning then turned to Eddie. "The staff thinks Dante is Nick. If Jameson is here, he might get spooked if he knows his dad is onto his trail. Plus, it makes more sense to the staff for me to bring my husband to the castle than to bring a random tattooed biker."

"Random?" Dante repeated. He raised his eyebrows.

"Bringing a *specific* tattooed biker isn't much better," I countered.

"Did Nick give his permission for this community theater sketch?" Eddie asked.

"Nick doesn't know and we're going to keep it that way." I turned around and yanked on the iron door handle. The door didn't budge. I put my foot on the brick for leverage and grabbed the handle with both hands. The door didn't budge. I turned back to them. "Any ideas?"

Eddie shook his head. We both looked at Dante. He reached into his pocket and pulled out a large black key, about twice the size of the one on Eddie's keyring. A fat black tassel hung from it. He fit the key into the door, turned it, and the tumblers fell. He held the door open. Maybe bringing a specific tattooed biker had been a good idea after all.

"Where did you—" Eddie started to ask, but I clamped my hand over his mouth before he could finish.

"Don't ask." I pointed my finger in Dante's face. "Don't tell."

The kitchen smelled of sage. A cast-iron skillet sat upside-down in a drying rack next to the sink. I led us through the room, feeling heat as we passed the oven. I turned back, yanked on the handle, and stuck my arm inside. The interior was still warm as if the oven had been in use not long ago.

"Madden asked the staff to take the day off," I said, "but someone used the oven this morning. Somebody else is here."

"Maybe it's Hans's ghost," Eddie said. He raised his fingers and wiggled them around. He opened the refrigerator and looked in. "A ghost who likes dressing."

"Salad dressing?"

"Thanksgiving dressing." He pulled out a Pyrex bowl.

It was covered in plastic wrap. He hugged the bowl to his chest and lifted the corner of the wrap, and a savory scent filled the room. "Marguerite is a treasure," he said. He plucked a bread cube out from the bowl and popped it into his mouth. Dante opened and closed a couple of drawers, finding the silverware. He pulled out a fork and speared some of the dressing for himself.

"This is breaking and *entering*, not breaking and *eating*." I pointed to the fridge. "Put that bowl back," I hissed at Eddie. "We don't want people to know we were here."

"You're right." Dante held his hand out. "Give me your keys. I'll move your car around back."

Reluctantly, I handed Dante the keys to my car. He propped the door open with a rock and left, and Eddie and I went inside.

We slowly made our way through the kitchen. I glanced back at the door twice, waiting for Dante to catch up with us. He could have told me to park out back when we got here, I thought. Just like a man, needing an excuse to get behind the wheel of my car.

As soon as the thought entered my mind, I knew Dante was gone. I ran out of the kitchen, through the bar, toward the front door. The skeleton key was in the lock, and I turned it and pulled. Sure enough, my car was missing.

"He took my car," I said.

"He's driving it around back like he said," Eddie said.

"You don't know Dante. Moving my car was an excuse. I don't know where he's going or what he's doing, but we're stuck here now."

"Then let's do what we came here to do."

I followed Eddie through the hallway to the staircase,

up the stairs, and down the hall to the archive room. As expected, the door was locked. He fit his key into the lock and opened it. I put my hand on his arm to hold him back before entering. "What about the motion detectors?"

"I was kidding about that. This isn't *Entrapment*."

He strode into the room and turned around. He held his arms out on either side. No alarms sounded. "It's temperature-controlled to protect the garments." He pointed to a small machine that was plugged in by the far wall. "Dehumidifier." He pointed to another small machine. "Air purifier." He wiggled his hips. "No motion detectors."

I opened a drawer on the table in the center of the room and pulled out a wad of white gloves. I took two and held the box toward Eddie. "Put them on."

"We're not here for the archives," he said. "You don't have to wear gloves to get the logbook."

"Have I taught you nothing? If someone stole a garment, they might have left evidence behind. We don't want to destroy fingerprints."

"If it was a member of the guild, they'd know to wear gloves."

"Right. If there *is* fingerprint evidence, then the police will have that much more to go on."

Eddie pulled on the gloves.

I stood back while he went to the file cabinet and opened the top drawer, fished inside, and pulled out a leather guestbook like the kind you find at weddings. He carried it to the table and flipped it open, then went page by page until he reached the end. I tried to conceal my impatience, though I secretly suspected he was going slow to drive me crazy.

"Here," he said. "Signed out by Hans a week ago." He pointed at the last entry in the book. "Totally legit."

I bent down and examined the line of handwriting. It followed the format to the preceding entries, with the garment description ("Levi's 501"), the date, and the name and signature of the person signing it out ("Hans Braeburn"). The initial field next to Hans's signature was blank.

I pointed that out to Eddie.

"Hans started the Fahrenheit Guild. He was above the rules. If he wanted to sign out his garment, nobody was going to stop him. Those jeans were always in rotation. Look." Eddie flipped back through the logbook to see other entries. The 501 was easy to find since the numbers made the entry stand out against descriptions like "Courrèges Boots," and "Réard Bikini." In each of the other cases where the 501 was written, the space for initials was left blank. "People love jeans," he said. "The Ribbon museum did a timeline of denim in 2005. There was a denim store on Penn Avenue that put this pair on display for their opening night, and the Philadelphia sewing society borrowed both the jeans and the piecework for one of their meetings."

"What a great concept," I said. "They wanted to see the individual pieces and the finished product."

For the first time since learning of the Fahrenheit Guild, I stopped to think about what could be studied and learned from the archives housed in this castle. It was one thing to go into a store and examine a garment. To touch the fabric, inspect the seams. Turn it inside out and analyze the construction. But it was another to see the individual pieces that would come together into a garment that was considered a classic. It was like seeing the paints used on the Sistine Chapel.

"How do people know about the guild? As far as I can tell, they're hush-hush and rely on word-of-mouth publicity. Someone should want to write about them."

"You're the style columnist for the paper," Eddie said.

"Yes, but I can't write about what I don't know."

"Maybe that's why you were asked to join."

"You're implying that someone wanted the guild to go public."

"A lot of members want the guild to go public. Hans was opposed, and since he was the founder, he was a big obstacle. From what Buck told me, Hans was never going to give in on that. But people get old, and the board forced him to consider a succession plan. Enter you."

"You said you nominated me, right?"

"Not exactly. I endorsed you. Different thing."

"How so?"

"The board already knew about you. You're famous enough around Ribbon that even people who don't care about fashion have heard of you. If they recruited you as a member, you'd be sworn not to leak information about the group. Insurance against negative publicity."

The items owned by the guild were arguably the foundation for every modern article of dress. But they remained secret, so someone would have to already be in the know before reaching out to access what was kept here.

"Can we look at the box again?"

"Why?"

"I don't know. When Ahn and I were here the other

day, I didn't know what I was looking for. Maybe I missed something."

Eddie shrugged. He put the logbook back into the cabinet and then moved the plexiglass panels out of the way and identified the box marked 501. He eased the box out of its space and carried it to the table. I took my position on the opposite side and we lifted the lid. Layers of tissue paper fluttered as we set the lid to the side, protecting nothing but an empty box. I'd secretly hoped the jeans had been returned, not because of the value of them, but because it would have told us something. But the jeans were still missing.

I put my hands inside the box and smoothed out the tissue on the bottom. There was a small lump in the corner. I ran my gloved hands over the tissue, and then flipped it up and pulled out a small plastic bag filled with leather patches.

"What's this?" I asked.

Eddie looked across the table. "Piecework," he said. "That belongs in the 501 box in the next room."

I stared at the bag. It was filled with a stack of Vachetta leather patches with red printing: the two-horse logo that was synonymous with Levi's jeans. "Why are there more than one?"

Eddie shrugged. "They probably correspond to different issues," he said. He pointed to my jeans. "You're wearing one version of the 501. Hans's is the 1944, but Levi's altered the pattern with the times and each variation is considered special."

I opened the bag and dumped the contents onto the stack of tissue paper we'd unpacked from the box, then sorted through the patches.

"What's on the back?" Eddie asked.

I flipped one over. A one-inch square black and white photo of a smiling man stared back at me. I'd never seen the man before, but a creepy realization of where the photo had come from sent a shiver through my body. I flipped the patches over and laid them across the table.

"Nineteen forty-four, nineteen fifty-five, nineteen sixty-six," I said slowly.

"You did your research."

"It's not research," I said. I held up the bag. "It's motive for murder."

"Hans?"

"Yes, but not how you think. This might be the evidence needed to prove Hans Braeburn murdered these men for their jeans."

25

SAME PAGE

I'd already filled Eddie in on a portion of what had been happening around the castle, and now I told him the rest. "If I'm right, then these patches correspond to the years that Levi's made significant changes to their pattern. I found yearbooks in the study that match up with those years too, and pictures have been cut out of each yearbook."

"Dude," Eddie said. *"Dude."* He pointed to the patches. "You have to call Madden."

"No," I said. Eddie started to protest, and I put my gloved hands up. "This isn't about Hans's murder. It's about Hans *being* a murderer. And what is it? Circumstantial at best. A stack of patches in a box where archival fashion materials are kept? He can't act on that. And the photos don't mean anything unless we can confirm the identity of the people pictured. Cecile Sézane is one of the people whose photo is missing, but she's alive and well, so my theory isn't exactly solid."

Eddie nodded, though he seemed to be in a bit of a trance. "You're right. You can't call Madden."

"But I *can* call Loncar."

HALF AN HOUR LATER, the empty 501 box was repacked with tissue and returned to its storage space, minus the bag of leather tags I'd found hidden amongst the tissue paper, and our white gloves were placed in the used glove box by the door. Once again, a Refraction Blue Toyota Supra was parked out front. An air of confidence seemed to have settled in on Loncar, and as he approached the castle door, he looked younger than his sixty-five-plus years. Maybe it was me being forty and seeing the world through older, wiser eyes that shifted my perspective.

"Thank you for coming," I said. "I didn't know who else to call."

I left Eddie upstairs in the archives and joined Loncar in the clubroom where I'd had my interview. We sat in the same chairs Detective Madden and I had occupied, but this time I chose the one Madden used.

"This will sound insane," I said. "I know that. And it might be. It might not matter to anybody but me, and it might seem like a bunch of crazy fashion stuff that you'll write off because I'm not a trained investigator, but I think there's something here. And I can't tell Madden, because anything I tell him, he'll have to investigate, and if I'm wrong, then he will have wasted his time."

"Ms. Kidd, what information do you have?"

I leaned back in my leather club chair and tapped my hand against the outside. At first, it was a steady beat, and then it shifted to finger drumming. I balled my hands up a few times and then released them, trying to work out the adrenaline rush that had left them tingling. Loncar's eyes moved from my face to my hands and back to my face. "Now you know how it feels."

"What is this?" I shook both hands as if flinging off water.

"Fight or flight reflex. The body sends warning signals to your hands and feet when you encounter information that indicates a threat. If you aren't confronted with a threat, you feel the sudden urge to move. It manifests in finger tapping and foot jiggling. Sometimes it helps to hold something."

"Like a pen?"

He nodded. I stood up and rolled the club chair closer to the row of tables, then grabbed a pen that had been left behind. Without thinking, I turned the pen around and started to tap it on the surface of the desk like I'd watched Loncar do a hundred times before. *Taptaptaptaptap.*

"Yesterday I was looking at yearbooks in the study. They had pictures cut out. Today, I was upstairs in the archives and found this bag of leather patches from the back of jeans." I slid the plastic bag toward him. "There are pictures attached to the back of each tag, and my hunch says the pictures match the holes cut out from the yearbooks."

"There's no crime in cutting out pictures and taping them to jeans labels," Loncar said.

"I know. But the yearbook years matched up with—" I stopped speaking abruptly. I'd shared a lot of ridiculous theories to Loncar over the years, but this was at the top of the list.

"Ms. Kidd," Loncar said. "You've suggested a lot of ridiculous theories over the years," (we always were on the same page!) "and while it sounded like the conjecture of a desperate person with an active imagination, I was duty-bound to check your information because it related to an open investigation."

"And you're a private detective now, so you can ignore whatever I say and leave."

"Your track record is surprisingly good," he admitted. "I'd like to hear what you have to say."

It was the nudge I needed. "The yearbooks match up with the years Levi's reissued their most iconic jeans. The pictures missing from the yearbooks match up with murder victims of unsolved cases that took place between here and Philadelphia. I think Hans Braeburn sought out men who were wearing the Levi's from that year—not reissues but the real thing—murdered them, and stole their jeans. Maybe the jeans were his trophy, or maybe the leather patch from the back was his trophy, but either way, I think it all links up."

I forced myself to look at Loncar. I expected to see doubt, humor, annoyance. I waited for the inevitable comment about how I was wasting his time. Loncar studied me but didn't respond. "I don't have a DNA kit, but I think this is pretty solid evidence."

He pulled the plastic bag of leather tags toward him. "These are the tags?"

"Yes."

"Where'd you find the yearbooks?"

"In the study."

"Show me."

"Madden took them."

"Show me where you found them."

I led Loncar to the study. The door was open the width of one cat. I'd expected Madden to have sealed it off with crime scene tape, but there was nothing to indicate we shouldn't enter. Still, I hesitated before putting my hand on the knob. Thanks to waking up on the sofa after being drugged and then finding Hans's body, the study was at the top of the list of creepiest spots in the castle.

I eased the door open, and we entered. The Tiffany light was on. An aluminum cup, like the kind you find in old camping gear, sat on the floor next to the sofa. Loncar picked it up and sniffed it. "Water," he said. He bent down and put his hand under the sofa, moved it to the side, and then pulled out an empty plate. "Was this for the cat?"

It could be. That was the thing. Everybody acted as if Wilhelm's comings and goings were perfectly normal. It wasn't outside the scope of possibility for Marguerite, or someone else, to have put a plate of food in the study for him. But I remembered the warm oven and the bowl of Thanksgiving dressing in the refrigerator. I took the plate from Loncar and sniffed it. It smelled faintly of sage.

I didn't answer Loncar. I turned away from him and stared at the bookcase. Leather-bound books sat in neat rows, organized alphabetically by author. The spot on the far right, where the out-of-order yearbooks had been, remained empty, but a heavy volume of Ray Bradbury short stories lay on its side on the shelf below. I wouldn't have noticed it if it had been there when I called Madden.

I slid a chair toward the bookcase and stood on it. Loncar held the chair in place. I picked up the unshelved book and slid it into the space on the bookcase where the missing yearbooks had been. I leaned against the book and pushed it in as far as it would go.

A mechanism started. At first, I thought it was my imagination. But Loncar let go of the chair and it moved, and I grabbed onto the bookcase for security. It wasn't my best idea. The bookcase was the object in motion, and as I clung to the shelf, it swung backward like a door, revealing a set of roughly carved stone stairs behind it.

Loncar grabbed me by the waist and lowered me to the ground. My heart was thumping in my chest. I put my hand on the bookshelf door and peered into the space revealed.

The hidden doorway was a surprise, but it wasn't the biggest of the moment. Because at the bottom of the stairs was a red-haired young man sitting on the dirt, hugging his knees. He looked up at me, and I down at him, and in that moment, I knew Dante's son Jameson had been found.

26

YEAH, OKAY

"You wait here." Loncar pushed me aside and went down the uneven stairs. There was no banister, but he kept one hand on the wall. The light in the basement was dim, coming from an unidentifiable light source. Loncar held his hand out to the kid, who took it and stood. I feared he was hurt or weak with hunger, but aside from the dirt and grime one might pick up while spending time in a hidden cellar in a castle, Jameson seemed unscathed.

Eddie returned to the study. "Is that a secret doorway?" he asked. His green eyes were wide with surprise.

"You've been to the castle before. You didn't know the bookcase moved?" He shook his head. I grabbed the aluminum cup and thrust it at him. "Go get some water."

Eddie left the room. By the time he returned, the teen was seated on the sofa. I took the cup from Eddie and handed it off. He held it on his knees but didn't drink.

I sat down next to him. "You're Jameson."

He nodded. He hung his head low, as if ashamed of

either his behavior or of having been caught. The one thing he didn't appear to be was grateful for having been rescued.

"You knew Regan. I saw your picture in the paper."

Jameson stared straight ahead. He had freckles across his nose, and his red hair flopped down on his forehead. The scruffy facial hair made him appear older than he was, but I questioned how I'd ever seen him as anything more than a teenager. He was scared and out of his element and didn't make eye contact with any of us.

"Jameson, these are my friends. Eddie Adams and Detective Loncar. We all know your dad. Do you mind if we call him?"

Jameson looked at me, then Eddie, then Loncar. Loncar nodded once, and Jameson looked back at me. "Yeah, okay."

I pulled out my phone and called Dante. "Yo," he answered."

"Jameson is here at the castle." The words came out in a rush. "I'm with Eddie. Loncar is here too."

Two days ago, Dante had been in bad shape. But this morning, he'd been his old self. I'd expected the news of his son would have a positive impact, but his voice remained modulated. "That's good. I'll be there shortly."

"Do you want to talk to him?"

There was no response, and I pulled the phone away from my head to check if the call had dropped, then took it off speaker. "I'm with Madden," he said, and I understood immediately.

Dante's reaction to the discovery of his missing son, or rather, lack thereof, made sense. If Jameson had been coming and going from the basement, using the hidden door to gain access to the castle interior, there would be evidence of his presence at the crime scene. When Madden collected the yearbooks, he may have found something else suspicious. He was investigating Hans's murder, and Jameson had means and opportunity.

"I'll meet you back at my house," I said. "Bring your motorcycle. Leave my car at your place—I'll get it later."

"Thank you," he said.

I hung up and looked at the men in the room with me. Two of them had an inkling of why this was a moral dilemma, but I could only predict one of their reactions.

"Which case are you investigating?" I asked Loncar.

"Mr. Lestes hired me to help find his son."

I felt the relief flood over me like a bucket of hot, soapy water. "Good." I turned to Jameson. "I think we all want to hear what you have to say, but would you be more comfortable talking to us if we moved this party to my house?" I asked. "There's a shower in it for you. Clean clothes, too."

"Yeah, okay."

Sometimes the universe conspires to make everything happen in your favor, and that's how finding Jameson felt. It might have been suspicious if Loncar and my matching cars were parked in my driveway, but Dante's "borrowing" had solved that problem. Dante being with Madden kept Madden from learning we'd found Jameson, which bought us time to get him out safely.

The self-help books were right. Sometimes things happened for a reason.

But something about the ease with which we'd found

Jameson, the visible aluminum cup, and the plate, felt careless. If Madden had seen those things, he would have scoured that room and found the hidden doorway, the staircase, and the missing teen. It was all too easy to think we'd been lucky. And that's why, before getting into the Loncar's Supra with Eddie and Jameson, I turned back toward the castle. "I need to check something," I said.

"Ms. Kidd," Loncar protested.

"I'll be a second." I ran back into the castle and returned to the study. The bookcase was closed. I got on the chair like before and jabbed my fingers into the vacant space until the mechanism tripped and the door swung open. I hopped down and wedged the chair into the opening (precautionary measure!), then descended the stairs carefully.

The room was lit by a small red camping oil lamp. It was the light source that had bothered me when we first opened the door. The cellar had no ventilation and no windows, but Jameson hadn't been sitting in the dark. He hadn't seemed scared, and he hadn't looked hungry, tired, hurt, or weak. I was beyond thrilled that he was okay, but I couldn't shake the feeling that this rescue hadn't been a rescue at all.

I had to leave. *We* had to leave. I could figure this out later if it mattered at all. The longer I remained, the more suspicious the others would get, or worse, the greater the chances the police would return while we were still on the castle premises.

Wilhelm slowly descended the stairs to join me. He rubbed his fur against the legs of my jeans, and then walked past me and jumped up on a black leather stool and curled into a ball.

"Come on, Wilhelm. You can't stay down here. I have to close the door behind me."

The cat raised his head and then lowered it again as if daring me to move him from his throne. I approached him and held out my hand. He sniffed my fingers, and then nuzzled me. I picked him up and held him against my chest while I started to leave, and then the familiarity of Wilhelm's chair hit home.

I turned back toward the black leather stool. The cushion wasn't covered in black leather, it was *draped* in black leather.

Black leather with flames.

I'd seen that black leather jacket hundreds of times in the past. I'd clung to it while riding on the back of a motorcycle around Ribbon.

Dante had been down here. He knew Jameson was hiding out at the castle. Our news, our big discovery, had been staged.

Freeing one hand, I reached out and pulled the garment off the stool. Wilhelm, probably not used to being held for long, wriggled against me to get free. He jumped down and ran.

"Wilhelm!" I called out. Anyone who's ever owned a cat knows I couldn't leave him trapped in the basement. Without fresh air, he wouldn't survive. I snapped my fingers and used the lantern to illuminate the corners of the room to find him.

The castle was silent. The stone walls blocked any sound from above. I pulled out my cell phone to call Eddie, but as expected, I had no signal. And as I spotted the fluffy tail of one gray and orange mottled-fur cat disappear behind a table, I heard wood snapping, followed by a whirring mechanism, followed by a heavy stone door slamming.

I raced back up the stone staircase but it was too late. The chair I'd used to prop open my exit had broken under the weight of the door and unless I found an inside release latch, I was trapped.

27

HUNCHBACK OF BRAEBURN CASTLE

THEY WOULDN'T LEAVE ME HERE.

That one positive thought ran through my head on repeat while my fingers searched the mortar around the door. Loncar and Eddie know I'm in here. They know I don't have a car. Loncar even watched me discover the door release, so he'd know how to get me out.

So where were they?

I went back down the stairs. The cellar was chilly, and I draped Dante's motorcycle jacket over the shoulders of my camelhair blazer. I held the red oil lantern and called out to Wilhelm.

"Come here, kitty," I said. "I won't leave you down here. I promise. You can trust me." I made the noises that Logan usually responded to and tiptoed across the dirty basement floor in the direction the castle cat had gone.

I found a wooden door about four feet high. I pushed on the door and it moved away from me, revealing a dark crawlspace. I held the lantern up. The ground was covered in threadbare rugs. Up ahead, I saw an opening into another room, but I was too far away to see what it was.

I crept inside. The door swung shut behind me. I moved slowly, bent at the waist with my back brushing against the roof of the passageway. It would have been easier to crawl, but if I dropped the oil lamp, I'd set the castle on fire, and not knowing how I was going to get out made fire a scary possibility. After about a hundred feet of impersonating the Hunchback of Braeburn Castle, I exited the crawlspace and entered a wine cellar.

A few feet ahead of me, Wilhelm meowed. Once he had my attention, he turned and trotted away. I followed him. He passed racks filled with bottles, oak casks, and wooden crates, reached another staircase, and went up. At the top, he lifted one paw and pushed against the inside of it and the door opened. He jammed his nose into the opening and wormed his way through.

I followed, the whole process a little easier since I was a person and not a cat. We were in the kitchen. Wilhelm trotted into the bar and lay down in the middle of a braided rug. This time, I let him sleep.

My cell phone buzzed with message alerts. I'd missed fourteen calls: thirteen from Eddie, two from Loncar, and one from an unknown number. Before I had a chance to listen to them, the kitchen door opened and Eddie rushed in.

"Dude, are you okay?"

"I got trapped in the basement. Let's go."

"We can't leave."

"Why not?"

"Loncar took Jameson to your place. I stayed here to figure out what happened to you. We don't have a car."

"So, what? We wait until Loncar comes back?"

"Yep, and it might be a while." He opened the refrigerator and pulled out the Pyrex bowl of stuffing. "You hungry?"

"Yes, but don't ask me to bring you a bottle of wine."

———

BY THE TIME we were rescued, Eddie had put a dent in the bowl of stuffing. I tried to meditate to calm my nerves, but my nerves had always been the one thing I could count on in terms of warning signs, and until I was safely home, I thought it better to leave my flight-or-flight instincts intact.

I assumed Wilhelm had food and water somewhere, but before we left, I put out a bowl of water and fresh food to be safe. We left him there and followed Loncar outside. Instead of the blue Toyota Supra, he was driving Nick's white pick-up truck.

"Is Nick here?" Eddie asked. He looked around the grounds.

"You left your car at my house," I said to Loncar, instantly understanding the logic behind the borrowed truck.

He nodded. "Get in."

We arrived at my house not long after. The Supra was in the driveaway, as was Dante's motorcycle. It was the beginnings of another house party.

I didn't know what to expect inside. Loncar's rescue mission had left Nick with Dante and Jameson. I trusted enough information would have passed between Loncar and Nick to bring Nick up to speed, but this whole situation had forced Nick and Dante together, not once, but twice.

The men were in the kitchen. Both Nick and Dante stood. I looked back and forth between their faces, something I'd been doing a lot lately. Nick's relief was written all over his. Dante, the most direct man I'd ever met in my life, was looking away. I already knew the secret Dante didn't want me to figure out. I'd deal with him later.

"Where's Jameson?" I asked.

"Upstairs," Dante said.

"In the shower," Nick added.

"He won't run away again," Dante said.

I was tired, not from physical exertion, but from the roller coaster of adrenaline I'd felt all day. I sat down and looked up at everybody. I didn't know who knew what, if anything. Nick, I felt certain, knew less than the rest of us, so I spoke directly to him.

"There's a room hidden behind the bookcase in the study at the castle," I said. "I triggered the release latch and the door opened. We found a staircase, and at the bottom we found Jameson."

"Hans was keeping him there?" Nick asked.

I ignored Nick's question and turned to Dante. "You knew," I accused. "How long?"

"I don't know what you're talking about."

I reached into my bag and pulled out Dante's leather jacket. I set it on the table in front of me and then looked up at him again. "I can place Jameson at the castle the night of the murder," I said. "He had means and opportunity. He and Hans had a fight, which may have led to motive. I don't know if your son is guilty of murder, but it's not going to help him if you lie to me."

Dante reached forward and picked up his jacket. He stared at it silently, as if wrestling with conflicting thoughts about how best to be a father figure. The rest of the men in the room stood still. The room was charged with tension: too much testosterone and not enough trust.

We'd all been focused on Dante, what he would say or do. I didn't expect him to leave, not while Jameson was upstairs, but I couldn't predict his next move either. I studied him and waited like the rest of the room.

After a long stretch of silence, Dante opened his jacket and draped it on the back of a chair. He put his hands on the chair back and leaned forward. "I didn't know until tonight," he said. "The dressing in the refrigerator. That was my mom's recipe. She made it every Thanksgiving, and now Cat makes it as our tradition. We walked into that kitchen and the smell of sage tripped a scent memory. When Eddie pulled the bowl out of the fridge, I knew exactly what it was."

"But if you found out when you tasted the stuffing, then how'd your jacket get into the basement?" Eddie asked.

It was then I noticed a second black leather jacket. It was draped over one of the stools by my breakfast nook. It had the same design painted on the back. Of course, Dante had more than one jacket.

"You gave him one," I suddenly said. "You gave Jameson a jacket like yours. The one I found is his. If I'd left it there, it would have been evidence."

I have a twisted sense of loyalty. My friends are my family, and I've gone to great lengths to protect them. But this time, it wasn't my friend in trouble, it was a stranger.

And my actions, taking Dante's jacket from the basement, had been proof to back up my accusation that Dante had known about Jameson's presence in the castle all along. By collecting the evidence I'd needed to catch Dante in a lie, I'd removed evidence that linked Jameson to the castle.

The worst thing wasn't that I felt guilty.

The worst thing was that Loncar, a former homicide detective who was tuned in to things like crime scene tampering, knew what I'd done.

"If he did it, he has to tell Madden," I said. "Not because it's the right thing to do, but because Madden and your sister are in a relationship."

Dante glared at me. I suspected if we all agreed to turn our backs for five minutes, Dante would have Jameson out of my house and I'd never see the kid again.

And then an unfamiliar voice spoke from the doorway. "I didn't kill Hans."

Dante turned around. Nick came to the back of my chair and put his hands on my shoulders, and Eddie leaned against the wall. Jameson stood at the threshold of the kitchen. His red hair stood up in wet spikes. He wore a T-shirt I recognized as one of Nick's and a pair of faded jeans that may have come from my does-not-spark-joy pile.

"I didn't kill him," Jameson said again. He scanned the faces in the room, lingering on Dante's, but then turning to mine. "but I know why he deserved to die."

LOOKING IN A MIRROR

"You don't have to do this," Dante said to his son.

I stood. "Yes, he does." I turned to Jameson. "You're young. You think you can keep a secret for the rest of your life, but you have no idea how long your life is going to be. You don't want to carry this around with you."

"You heard him say he didn't do it," Dante snapped. "Jameson isn't guilty of murder."

"No, but Hans was." I turned to Jameson. "Wasn't he?"

Jameson looked scared. The front of his hair flopped against his forehead. His eyes were rimmed in red. I didn't know Jameson, but today I recognized something familiar. I saw a teen who argued with his mother, got drawn into fights in the park, and acted out in school. I also saw a kid in a room of adults, scared that he was going to be punished for something he said or something he did.

Instinctively, I put my hand on his arm. "You're safe here. Everybody in this room wanted to make sure you were okay." I didn't turn to look at Loncar, the one wildcard. He told me he'd been hired to find Jameson, and Jameson was found, and that was good enough for me.

Jameson held my stare. I smiled. I felt an urge to make sure he knew he could trust me. And the only way I knew to do that was to offer him something none of the others could.

"Can I talk to Jameson alone?" I asked. I scanned the faces of the men in the room. Nick looked understanding. Eddie looked scared.

"I don't like it," Dante said. That wasn't a no.

Loncar was the one to surprise me. "Give them space."

I waited until the others went outside. Maybe Loncar was going to show off his engine block. I turned my full attention to Jameson. "Let's sit down."

We took chairs opposite each other in the living room. "I'm Samantha," I said. "I met your aunt about seven years ago. It was after I moved into this house. I moved here from New York and started a job, and then my new boss was murdered on my first day. I'm the one who found his body."

"Where?" he asked.

"In an elevator." It was the kind of experience you don't realize you'll think about again and again, until one day you wake up and realize that was the day your life changed forever. "I didn't do the right thing. EMTs took him out of the building, and I tried to go about my day. It was a new job, and I was already nervous. I tried to pretend nothing had happened."

"How'd that go?"

"You know the older man out there?" I asked, pointing toward the door. Jameson nodded. "He was the homicide detective investigating the case," I said. A look of fear passed across Jameson's features. He put his hands on the arms of the chair and gripped tight enough to make his skinny fingers go white. "It's okay. He's a private investigator now. Your dad hired him to help find you."

"But *you* found me."

"I have a knack for things like this." I gave him a wry smile. "I spent a miserable week hiding from the police while my boss's killer tried to frame me. The longer I avoided telling anybody what I knew, the worse I made things for myself. It wasn't until I talked to him," I jerked my thumb toward the front door, "that things turned a corner."

"Did he catch the killer?"

Technically, I did that too, but this didn't seem the time for bragging rights. "The killer was eventually caught, yes."

"And your life went back to normal?"

Not exactly. "Sort of." We were getting off track! "The point is, I made things worse by trying to keep a secret I had no reason to keep. I wasn't guilty. You're not guilty. But you know things about that night. You were there. I know you're scared, but you're not the bad guy here."

Jameson studied me, and then looked at the table. He stared at the leather jacket I took from the hidden room. He reached forward and pulled it off the table, and I felt the tickle of despair. Being honest with him hadn't worked. He was going to put on his jacket and leave and this time, none of us would know where he ran to.

He unfolded the jacket and reached into the inside pocket. He pulled out a worn Vachetta leather patch with red printing. It was the tag from a pair of Levi's like the others I'd found with Eddie. Jameson set the patch on the placemat between us.

"That came from Regan's jeans."

"How did you get it?"

"Hans killed him. He didn't know I was there, or that I saw anything. He killed Regan and then took his jeans and left. I got scared. I thought he was going to come after me next, so I hid. Hans put the jeans in his car and drove away. I took Regan's car followed him."

"You're fourteen."

"I'm not a kid," he said defensively. "I know how to drive."

"Go on."

"I followed Hans to Ribbon. I ditched Regan's car in a used lot about half a mile away and hiked back to the castle. I snuck inside when the maid was airing out the carpet in the hallway, and I found Regan's jeans in the study. I knew they were his because his name was on the inside of the waistband."

"Is that a thing?" I asked. "I thought that's what parents did when they sent their kids off to camp."

"Regan said somebody was going around Philly mugging guys for their jeans. Sounded crazy, but then my mom warned me about staying out late. Something about some kids found unconscious in their underwear." He shook his head and fingered the patch. "This was on the desk at the castle. I don't know why I took it."

"Insurance," I said.

"Huh?"

"A part of you knew that patch connected Hans to your friend and as long as you had it, Hans wouldn't hurt you."

"Regan wasn't my friend. He was a guy who dealt drugs in my neighborhood. He tried to recruit me, and my mom found out. She grounded me. I snuck out my window and told Regan I wasn't going to work for him. We got into a fight. I came home with a busted lip and a black eye, and my mom said she was done trying to raise me, and I was going to live with my dad. The day I was supposed to move in with him was the day Hans killed Regan—"

"—and you never made it to your dad's house."

Jameson looked away. "I planned to call my dad when things settled down, but then somebody murdered Hans. I was already in trouble, and nobody knew I was here." He glanced at me. "Nobody but you."

"How did you find out about the secret room?"

"Do you know about Alfred?"

For a moment, I was thrown off. "Bruce Wayne's butler?"

Jameson dropped his chin to his chest and for the first time since we'd started talking, he grinned. "There's an app that turns your cell phone into a surveillance camera. I set up an account for my mom. Hans spent most of his time in the study, so I set up my cell phone to see what he did in there."

"I don't follow."

"You login from a computer and access the camera from an internet browser."

"Where did you log in?"

"I had my laptop in Regan's car." He seemed defensive. "There's a diner down the street with an open internet signal."

Despite Dante not having a regular presence in Jameson's life, the apple hadn't fallen far from that tree. I thought about how Jameson's attitude and skills were nature, not nurture, and how something as abstract as investigative prowess and curiosity had gotten coded into his genes.

"You saw him go into the secret room behind the bookcase."

"I knew it had something to do with the yearbooks. He used a cane, but I didn't know where he kept it, so I climbed onto a chair and pulled down the yearbooks and saw the mechanism. I pushed it, and the door swung in, and after that, I had a place to stay."

"How did you find out the hidden room was connected to the wine cellar?"

"Wilhelm," he said. "The first time he showed up, he scared me. I was down there and the door was closed and suddenly, there's this cat who is very much alive. After I realized he had a way to come and go, I followed him."

I nodded. Everything Jameson said fit the narrative. He was probably the one to put the yearbooks back on the shelf out of order, and that was what first drew my attention to the bookcase.

"You know I was at the castle the night Hans was murdered," I said. "I saw you and Hans." I stopped talking and allowed that statement to balloon and trigger an angry outburst, but it elicited nothing more than a nod. "You two argued, and Hans hit you. What was that about?"

"Earlier that day, Hans found out I was there."

"Did you tell him what you knew?"

"No. I said I was a runaway. He asked how old I was, and I told him."

Fourteen. He was a kid. Here was a boy who'd watched

a ninety-five-year-old man kill someone he knew, who'd followed him to seek justice. It was either brave or stupid —I couldn't decide which. It was like looking in a mirror.

"Weren't you scared?"

Jameson stared at the toes of his sneakers. He propped the heel of his right foot on top of the toe of his left. I figured if the answer was no, he wouldn't have taken a sudden interest in his shoes. Again, like looking in a mirror.

"He wanted me to hide. That night, when he saw me in the study, he ordered me to get back down in the basement. I said no. I told him I knew what he did to Regan, and I was going to the cops. That's when he slapped me."

Considering what Hans was capable of, the slap felt out of character.

"He said something to you. He said, 'watch yourself, or you'll be next.' What did he mean?"

Jameson looked up, and his deep brown eyes were wide. Any brave pretense fell. "Hans said he never killed anyone under eighteen. That was where he drew the line. When he first caught me, he said I was lucky I was fourteen, I wasn't worth the hassle."

Eighteen. It was the age Hans was when he first moved to the United States. Was that symbolic?

It seemed inconceivable that Hans was behind the murders Carl mentioned and the recent wave of jean jackings in Philadelphia, but Jameson's story connected it all. He was a witness to Hans's recent crime, and the patch from Regan's jeans was just like the bag of patches I'd found that connected to the victims in the yearbooks.

I had yet to discover one redeemable thing about Hans Braeburn, and the more I learned, the more convinced I was that there was nothing to be found. Even his obsession with denim was linked to the crimes he'd committed. The guild merely gave him a forum to display what he'd amassed through a streak of serial murders.

I had one last question, and I felt if I didn't press the issue now, I'd never know for sure. "Why didn't you hide in the basement like Hans asked?"

"If I didn't do anything, he was going to get away with it. I knew he wouldn't hurt me while all those people were there, so I stood up to him. When everybody went to the meeting, I went to the kitchen to get something to eat. I heard someone in the wine cellar, and I took off out back."

"Who was in the wine cellar?"

He shrugged. "Probably the person who killed Hans. I don't know who it was. I didn't stick around to find out." He looked up at me, and for the first time since I'd met him, I was struck by how familiar his deep brown eyes were, how they weren't the root-beer-barrel shade of Nick's, but the velvety dark chocolate shade of Dante's. It was his red hair that had kept me from seeing the resemblance between him and Dante. When I'd met him, I hadn't even known Dante's son was missing.

I stared past Jameson into a corner of the dining area, letting memories of that first night at the castle come back to me. Hans's confrontation with Jameson. My interview. Getting drugged. Waking up on the sofa in the study, finding Buck and Lucy in the bar, and discovering Hans's body while on my way to leave.

"Wait here," I said.

I stood and opened the front door, then beckoned the men back inside. The night was cool, and with them came a burst of crisp air that cooled the living room considerably. I rubbed my hands over my arms to stave off the chill and gathered them around.

"Here's what we're going to do," I said. I pointed at Loncar. "You give Dante and Jameson a ride to Dante's house. Dante, bring my car back here and get your motorcycle. I'll take Eddie home. Nick stays. If Madden comes over, it needs to look like one of us is here."

To their credit, they listened to me. But before we could put our plan into action, the doorbell rang. Nick was closest to the door. He stood from the overstuffed chair and looked out the peephole, then opened the front door.

"Detective Madden," he said. "We've been expecting you."

29

HOSTESS WITH THE MOSTESS

I FORCED A SMILE. IF WE'D BEEN EXPECTING DETECTIVE Madden, it was because we anticipated complications. Madden came in, followed by Dante's sister, Cat. She grinned broadly when she saw me, and I rushed forward and threw my arms around her.

"We were on a date," she said, hugging me back. "I called Dante to see if he'd heard anything, and he mentioned he was here, so I thought it would be fun to surprise you both." She turned her head and studied her brother. "Surprise."

Cat was one of those women who look perfectly put together all the time. Her bright lipstick never bled into the cracks around her lips, and her striking red hair was never out of place. These days, she'd gone shorter than when I first met her, sporting a layered Jean Seberg pixie. Most women would fear it made them look like a boy, but on Cat it was sexy. I could tell from how Madden looked at her he agreed.

Tonight, she wore a purple knit dress that showed off

the curves she'd developed after becoming a mother. She topped it with a pink double-faced cashmere wrap coat, sheer pink pantyhose, and pink suede pumps and carried a bright blue handbag. Cat's fashion sense had always been edgy, and after a week surrounded by jeans, I found I was jealous.

"Who wants a nightcap?" Nick asked. He stood in the doorway between the living room and the kitchen and held up a bottle of B&B.

"I'll have one," Cat said.

"Me too," Eddie chimed in. Loncar shook his head. Dante stood and approached Nick. "I'll help carry the glasses."

"Can you get another bottle from the basement?" Nick glanced at the door that led to the cellar. It was open. "There's a case next to my desk."

"Sure," Dante said. He strode past Nick, not even glancing at the dining room table where Jameson had sat. To anyone who'd been there before Madden and Cat arrived, it was obvious why. The important part was to make sure everybody acted naturally, and the best way to do that was to be the hostess with the mostess.

Idle chitchat filled the room while Nick and Dante left. Nick returned shortly with a tray of drinks. He circulated the room and distributed them.

When he reached me, he said, "Take Cat upstairs and show her what you've been working on."

Cat's eyes lit up. "You have a project? Show me!"

Did Nick not understand how important it was for us to keep Madden from discovering Jameson was here? Did he not see how tenuous Jameson's freedom was? Or how one false step would blow the whole operation?

"Go ahead," Madden said to Cat. He kissed her temple. "I know how much you miss talking fashion with Samantha."

She beamed at him, and I felt a pang of conflict.

I led Cat up the stairs to the spare bedroom. I'd forgotten the condition in which I'd left the room. Piles of clothes were strewn about, and the room was no closer to being organized or emptied than when I first started the project.

Cat stood in the doorway. Her eyes moved from pile to pile. "The Life-Changing Magic of Tidying Up," she guessed.

"How did you know?"

"I went through the same phase when I sold my house."

I kicked a path through the piles on my way to the desk. There weren't a lot of surfaces on which to sit, but I emptied two chairs on opposite sides of the desk, and we took positions as if Cat were interviewing me in a very messy office.

"My brother won't talk to me about Jameson," Cat said. "He doesn't trust me."

"Was it your idea to come here tonight?"

She dropped her head in shame. "Jameson is my nephew," she said. "He's my daughter's uncle. He's a good kid, and I'm worried about him."

"Jameson may have gotten mixed up in something dangerous."

"Did he?" She lifted her head and stared directly at me. "Do you know where he's at?"

"No," I answered, relieved that it was the truth. Jameson had been in my kitchen less than an hour ago, but he seemed to vanish the moment Madden and Cat showed up. I had no idea where he'd gone, but I hoped beyond hope he hadn't thought we set him up.

"I know you, Samantha. I know you as well as my brother knows you and maybe even better. You don't let things like this go. You're helping him, right? You're doing what you can to find him?"

"Cat…"

She sniffled. "He's a fourteen-year-old boy. He acts tough like Dante used to, but he's a just kid."

I wanted to tell her it was okay, we'd found him, he was going to be fine. I wanted to let her know she didn't have to worry anymore. But her and Detective Madden's arrival had put a kink in the evening, and I no longer knew if any of what I wanted to tell her was true.

"How is your baby?" I asked.

"She's three," she said. She smiled. "She talks. I asked her what she wanted for her birthday and she said cashmere."

"She *didn't*."

"She said 'ka-me,' and pointed to my chunky lime green cashmere sweater, so I'm pretty sure she did."

"Are you giving it to her?"

"You try resisting a three-year-old girl asking for cashmere."

I smiled at the thought. Maybe someday I'd have a three-year-old girl asking me for cashmere. Or maybe she'd want little Gucci loafers. Maybe we could have matching outfits! Or maybe…it would be a boy. I had no idea what I would do with a boy.

At least Gucci loafers were unisex.

Cat spent the next few minutes filling me in on her

daughter's antics. The only time I'd ever seen Cat not thrive was when she was eight months pregnant, and one could argue that's not the finest hour for most women.

"What about you?" she asked.

"Me?" I longed to tell her my news, but until the doctor gave me a clean bill of health, Nick and I had agreed to keep it to ourselves. "I'm staying busy with the column for the paper and helping out around the house."

"How long are you going to go on like this?"

"Like what?"

"Samantha, every article of clothing you've ever bought is on the floor of your spare bedroom. You're still looking for something. You've been looking for something since I met you. Maybe what you're looking for isn't in this house."

"Nick and I have never been better," I said.

"I'm not talking about Nick. You guys are perfect together. Even this thing with Jameson—Dante told me how much Nick's been helping, and that's because of you and what you do. But it won't always be like this," she said. "Life moves and shifts and changes, and we're supposed to move and shift and change with it."

I picked up a T-shirt from a pile close to me. It had originally been black, was now faded, and had a metallic iron-on that said, THE KID. I'd bought it oversized during a childhood vacation at the Jersey shore and continued to wear it long after it was age-appropriate. The decal was peeling off on one corner, and the copper metallic was almost white. I flashed back to that summer, stalking T-shirt shops with my family, seeking out the perfect option to capture the memories of my nine-year-old self.

"I'm not like you," I said. "I always have one foot in hot

mess and another in crazy town. I'm irresponsible, impulsive, and disorganized." I set the T-shirt on top of the desk and smoothed out the wrinkles. "I flit from one thing to the next. I don't even know if I'd recognize true happiness if I had it."

"Is that why you're tidying?" She gestured to indicate the mess in the room.

"Fashion makes me happy. These clothes are part of that. But it's like a museum around here. Most of these garments are things I've kept because they remind me of where I was when I wore them, not because I expect to wear them again."

"You majored in fashion history, right?"

"Right."

"Your entire degree was based on the notion that our clothes reflect our lives. They're no different than art, or musical styles, or literary trends. That doesn't mean you're a bad person for not wearing them forever."

Cat pulled my THE KID T-shirt toward her. She flipped it over so the decal was face-down. She folded the left side in, then the right, folded the hem up about a third of the way, and then folded the neckline down. She doubled that over itself until the T-shirt was shaped like a tight tube.

"Did it work for you?" I asked. "Tidying up?"

She handed me the T-shirt. "Yes, but not until I realized tidying up wasn't about closet space."

AFTER SPELUNKING through some of the more unusual garments on the floor, Cat and I returned to the living room. The makeshift party had unusual energy. Eddie and

Detective Madden were looking at a book on skateboard culture. Dante and Nick were next to each other on the sofa. The TV was on, and Loncar appeared to be the only one watching the game.

Madden looked up when he saw us. He set his still-full glass on a coaster and stood. "It's getting late," he said. "We should be going."

Cat looked at Dante. "Call me if you hear anything about Jameson," she said. Dante held her gaze and then nodded once. He shifted his eyes from her to me and back to her. I didn't move. We were *this close* to making it through the evening, and there was no point in spilling Jameson's secret now.

"I'm okay, Aunt Cat," said a voice behind me. I turned to face the voice. The door that led down to the basement opened, and Jameson spilled his secret himself.

30

DOES NOT SPARK JOY

SUDDENLY, IT WAS PANDEMONIUM. DANTE SPRUNG FROM his seat and rushed toward Jameson. Nick turned to Madden. Eddie knocked over his drink. And Loncar leaned forward and peered through the legs of the people in his way to check the score of the game.

Everybody spoke at once. It took me standing on the ottoman and piercing the noise with a sharp whistle to get their attention. I didn't know how it looked to Detective Madden but considering it *might* look as if five people were at my house conspiring to hide a person of interest in a recent homicide, I thought it best to take the temperature of the room. And the problem with having gotten everyone to shut up and look at me was that now I had to figure out what to say.

That problem was quickly solved. "You knew?" Cat asked, whirling on me. "I asked you if you knew where he was, and you lied. You knew he was here." Her eyes flashed with anger, hurt, and tears, and I couldn't blame her.

"I'm sorry," I said. "I didn't know—"

"Stop lying, Sam. He was in your *basement.*" She turned to Jameson. "You're okay?"

He looked more scared of her than he'd been when I first found him in the castle. "Yes, Aunt Cat."

"Call your mother and tell her that." She looked at Detective Madden. "I want to leave." She pulled on her coat and stormed out the front door.

Madden, to his credit, didn't seem conflicted. He grabbed his jacket from the arm of the sofa and followed her outside. A few seconds later, an engine started, and a few seconds after that, a car backed out of my driveway.

We all stood like that for about a minute. I kept thinking Madden would walk back in, that maybe he'd given his keys to Cat and told her he had to do his job. He didn't.

"I'm sorry, Dad," Jameson said to Dante. "I didn't do anything wrong. I don't want to hide anymore."

Wordlessly, I watched Dante approach Jameson. If Dante had been the one hiding, he would have stayed in the basement. No, that wasn't true. Dante would have ducked out the back door and taken off again, this time doing a better job of covering his tracks. He would have been drawn back to the castle to try to catch the real murderer. And here was his son, so like him in his spirit and attitude, yet so different when it came to this. I braced myself for an argument that I had no right to witness.

Dante put his arms around Jameson and hugged him. All the fight drained from the boy as he collapsed against his dad. He hugged back. It was a deeper show of intimacy and love than I'd expected to see and I turned away. Eddie, Nick, and Loncar all had tears in their eyes.

THE PARTY BROKE UP. Now that the Madden Factor was no longer a concern, everybody wanted to go home. Loncar gave Eddie a ride to the restaurant where he'd left his VW Bug, and Dante took Jameson to his apartment on his motorcycle. Nobody offered to bring my car back to my house, and I was too tired to care. I'd gone without wheels before, and I could do it again.

Loncar and Eddie left first. While Jameson was putting on the spare helmet, Dante lingered behind. "Thank you, Samantha."

"For what? The cops are probably waiting at your house, and your sister is so mad she probably won't talk to me again."

"Cat's not mad at you."

"Didn't you see that outburst? I'm pretty sure she is."

"Nah." He shrugged into his leather jacket. "I'm pretty sure she's mad at me, but she'll get over it. That tantrum was her way of getting Madden out of here."

"You don't mean she planned that."

"Probably not a plan, but she's a mom now. Her loyalties are with her family."

"Could that break them up?"

"You saw how he looked at her." Dante stared at the door. "Don't worry, Samantha. Madden will have Jameson's statement by this time tomorrow."

It sounded like a solid intention. He may have even

believed it. But I couldn't help wondering if I'd ever see the two of them again.

After clearing the living room, Nick went to bed. I promised to be along shortly but was too wound up to sleep. I went to the spare bedroom and read about the life-changing magic of tidying up. Cat was right; it had nothing to do with closet space.

I sorted my way through the night with a new filter in place. Not that of a fashion archivist who bestowed significance on every garment ever worn, but a person who surrounded herself with so much stuff from the past she could barely see beyond it to the possibility of the future.

The black pinstriped pantsuit I'd purchased at Cat's store to wear to my first industry event in Ribbon: does not spark joy.

The black suit I'd gotten with my clothing allowance during a short stint at a flash-in-the-pan retailer: does not spark joy.

The blue camouflage pants I had on the night I found Cat's husband's body: does not spark joy.

The leopard-printed suit I bought to blend in with the local mafia wives: does not spark joy.

The panties I'd worn while flashing the crowd at a lingerie show in Las Vegas ... okay. They sparked a *little* joy.

I finished somewhere after four a.m. Twenty-five trash bags of clothes lined the wall by the closet. Neater piles, ones that contained my all-time favorites, were on the opposite side of the room. I'd found some treasures amongst my belongings and even a couple of things that still had tags.

I pulled the door closed behind me and went to bed. Logan was asleep in the middle of my side. I shifted him down and curled up next to Nick, falling asleep moments later.

When Nick's alarm went off two hours later, it tore me from a dreamless sleep. "Stay put, Kidd," he said. He got up and I pulled myself into the center of the bed and dropped back to sleep. When I woke again, the sunlight was streaming into the room, bathing Logan in a soft, natural glow against his black fur. He licked his paw and wiped it over his face. I turned myself around so I was face to face with him and stroked his fur on his head. He stopped cleaning himself and meowed, and then stood up and head-butted me. I wrapped my arms around him and held him against me until he wriggled free, jumped down, and left the room.

I got up, showered, and dressed in a white T-shirt trimmed with tweed at the collar and sleeves and a pair of designer boot-cut jeans. Unlike the pair of Nick's I'd borrowed yesterday, these were loaded with stretch. I laced on a pair of black patent leather combat boots. There was something about the juxtaposition of masculine and feminine, of tough and soft, that suited my mood.

I blow-dried my hair and pulled it back into a low ponytail, put on a little makeup, and went looking for Nick. His truck was missing, and the driveway was empty.

I was still stranded.

I went back inside. The newspaper was spread across the table. I grabbed a mug of coffee and sat. On the front page was an article by Carl Collins. *Suspect Held in Connection to Murder at Braeburn Castle.*

Everybody at the castle knew Jameson had been found, but who had told Carl? The last thing I'd been privy to was Dante and Jameson leaving together. It had been late. The paper goes to bed at eleven. Even if Carl had been lurking around my house spying through the windows, he wouldn't have known Jameson was there until far beyond the deadline. I pictured him yelling "Stop the presses!" but then I pictured our editor's expression and Carl saying, "Just kidding, it can wait until tomorrow."

Besides, what did it mean, "suspect held?" Madden hadn't arrested Jameson.

As I pulled the paper closer, I realized while I'd learned a lot over the past twenty-four hours, what I'd learned was just the tip of the iceberg.

The suspect wasn't Jameson. It was billionaire Buckley Owen Hollinger the Fourth.

31

SYMPATHETIC BILLIONAIRE

I READ THE ARTICLE TWICE AND CALLED CARL. "IT'S Samantha," I said. "Where did you get the scoop about Buck Hollinger?"

"Buck Hollinger the Fourth," he said. "Our legal team says it's very important to say his full name any time we mention him."

"He's in custody?"

"I got a tip from the police. The cops picked up BH-four last night after a key piece of evidence was dropped off at the police station. Something about the results of the victim's blood-alcohol test and the suspect's recent travel records."

"You lost me."

"Buck Hollinger the Fourth was in Austria last month. That's one of two countries where you can obtain Rohypnol with flunitrazepam, which was the drug found in the victim's system when the autopsy was done. The drug works on the central nervous system, which probably either killed the victim or paralyzed him so he couldn't fight back."

"What was the cause of death?"

"His heart stopped."

"But why?"

"He was a ninety-five-year-old man who ingested a sizeable amount of an illegal substance. I don't think the police are looking for a smoking gun."

I felt equal parts sick to my stomach and angry. Buck had been careless in his distribution of the drug, and I'd been as much of a victim as Hans.

But Hans Braeburn wasn't a victim. He was a murderer. Jameson's statement said as much. Carl's article mentioned nothing about Hans's connection to the jean jackings or the string of victims he'd left in his wake. That was as much a part of the story as anything else.

"What have you found out about Hans?" I asked Carl.

"Haven't we covered this? Lived in that creepy castle for the past seventy-seven years doing who knows what. He probably has a stash of bodies buried out back."

"Why'd you say that?"

"Think about it, Kidd. People like Hans Braeburn don't change their spots, they find better ways to hide them. The world is rid of one bad man. I'm not one for vigilante justice, but Buck Hollinger the Fourth did a good thing when he killed Hans Braeburn. Buck Hollinger the Fourth might be the most sympathetic billionaire the world has ever seen."

And that was exactly why I didn't believe he did it.

I FELT like I knew more than I knew. I'd been at the castle when Hans died. The drugs in my system had compromised my memory, though my relatively fast recovery left me confused as to what the drugs had done. I hopped online and read what I could find on benzodiazepines. The research led me to a string of additional facts, and within half an hour, I was an expert on the subject. It was like cramming for a final exam, and I suspected the newly acquired knowledge would fade from my memory in a day or two so I had to act fast.

I called Dante. "Did you see the paper?" I asked when he answered. "Jameson's in the clear. There's another member of the guild in custody for Hans's murder. Jameson already said he didn't see who killed Hans, so he's not at risk anymore."

"I'm not taking that chance."

"You're not in Ribbon anymore, are you?"

"I'm taking Jameson home."

Dante's present tense, combined with what I knew about Dante, led me to an unfortunate conclusion. "You took my car."

"I'll bring it back."

"You took my car?"

"Samantha—"

"It's one thing for you to 'borrow' it at the castle. That worked out for us. But now? I'm stranded. And it's new. And—"

"—and I'll bring it back after I drop him off at his mother's house. This was the only way to keep him safe."

I narrowed my eyes and bit my lip. Dante was manipulating me based on my penchant to protect people. "Don't get into any accidents," I said, "And I expect it returned with a full tank of gas." I hung up.

In the time between losing my last car and buying the current one, I'd been a vehicular burden on every person I knew. Both Eddie and Nick had gotten used to carting me around town, but they both had lives. I'd made friends with a taxi driver who had expanded his services to Uber, Lyft, and airport-shuttling, but even though I tipped generously, he was so busy he wasn't available at the drop of a hat. I considered keeping a driver on the payroll, but the vetting process to find someone willing to tolerate the scrapes I got into took longer than a twenty-minute interview.

The problem wasn't that I was stranded at home, it was that I didn't know which direction to turn. If the police were right, then Hans's murder was solved. And after everything I'd learned about Hans, I couldn't say I cared as much about catching his killer as I had in other cases. I'd been more concerned with finding Jameson and making sure he was safe, and he was.

Even the idea of replacing Hans in the Fahrenheit Guild was tarnished now that I knew about the murders he might never be charged with committing. It was the most frustrating case I'd been involved with because there was no justice to be had.

I tore open a bag of Multigrain Splits and carried them to the table. I ate half the bag while I flipped through the rest of the newspaper. I opened a new document on my laptop and started an article about jeans, not the usual history of, but a beginner's guide.

Five days ago, when I first learned I was to become the 501 expert, I'd felt let down. Jeans were jeans, I'd thought.

I knew differently now. I'd thought all Levi's were the same, but even the ones they sold at the big-box stores came from five different countries and each used a slightly different quality fabric. Then there were things like selvedge, denim weight, leg shape, and the history of the red tab. Even the arcuate—the stitching on the back pocket—varied from the jean's inception until now. During World War II, when rationing of raw materials affected the whole country, the arcuate was painted on and not stitched, to conserve thread.

Wait. A. Minute.

The piecework of jeans that were in the archives of the guild was supposed to be from 1944. That was the jean style I'd been recruited to memorize. But the preserved sample was missing. I hadn't been able to examine it. And of the individual components of the jeans that were in the piecework archives, the back pocket pieces in the parts box of the deconstructed jeans, had stitching. Those pockets couldn't have been original. Why would the guild founder, the person responsible for honoring the history of an item, keep anything other than the original in the archive room?

It meant something. It *had* to. Except it sounded ridiculous even to me, claiming the stitching on a back pocket of a pair of deconstructed jeans was a clue to a murder. It very well might have been the craziest thing I'd ever considered saying out loud.

And I'd said a lot of crazy things out loud.

I retrieved my phone from the counter where it had been charging since last night and called the person I should have called the first time. Detective Loncar.

"It's Samantha Kidd," I said. "I'd like to hire you to

investigate a stolen pair of jeans." I held my breath and waited for a response. When there was none, I continued. "I'll pay your regular retainer and your daily expenses, and I'll get you access to whatever you need."

"Were these jeans being housed at Braeburn Castle?" he asked.

"Yes. I know you recently closed a case with a missing teenager that resulted in the arrest of a person of interest in a homicide. This may be related to that. I don't know yet. But if it is, I don't think the right person is in custody. Will you take the case?"

"Do you have access to the castle?"

"Yes."

"Jameson Lestes is safe?"

"For now."

"Okay," Loncar said. "This one's on the house."

We'd come a long way since that first case when I'd thought Detective Loncar was A) a bumbling police detective and B) out to get me. We'd developed an unbreakable bond (my words), collaborated regularly (my exaggeration), and might someday become partners (my wishful thinking).

I left a note for Nick, cleaned Logan's litter box, and ate a few more pretzels. I was darn close to finishing the bag, so I pulled on a leather blazer and waited on the front porch for Loncar to arrive. The sight of the Refraction Blue Supra coming down the street gave me a thrill even though it wasn't my car.

I didn't give Loncar time to turn the engine off. I approached the passenger side and lowered myself into the black leather seat moments later.

Loncar glanced at my legs. "You're back to cheap jeans," he said.

"These are Hudson," I said dismissively. "They weren't cheap. They cost a hundred and ninety-five dollars."

He glanced at me, and then backed out of my driveway and drove toward the castle. "You paid for the label, not the denim."

"Designer jeans aren't like heritage jeans. I paid for the cut, the wash, and the fit." I smoothed out the factory-faded denim over my thighs. "They fit me perfectly." I considered pointing out how great they made my butt look, but this was Detective Loncar, and that was unfamiliar territory.

"For now, they do. They probably lose their shape half an hour after you put them on."

He was right. How was he right? "How did you know that?"

"I like jeans," he said. "I've been wearing them since I was a kid. After a while, I recognized the ones produced today aren't as good as the ones I used to wear, so I went out looking for ones that were."

I turned in my seat and stared at him. "Who are you and what have you done with my detective?"

Loncar smiled a rare smile. "You're not the only person around here with a curious mind."

I glanced down at his legs. The jeans he wore were faded, but the color of the denim down the side seam of the jean was darker. "Are those selvedge?"

He nodded. "I've had this pair since I graduated from the academy."

"What was that, 1955?"

He glared at me. "1974."

He turned off the main road onto the narrow one that accessed the castle. A faint memory tickled my mind. "I thought you wore Wranglers."

"I do. Different camp than Levi's folks. Not as much of a crossover with hipsters."

"I wonder why that is?"

"Wranglers were associated with the rodeo crowd. Levi's went the other direction. Once an identity gets infused into your brand, it's hard to shake. Levi's went into reproductions of their classic styles before any of the other denim vendors and that drew in a new audience."

"You never thought about switching brands?"

He shrugged. "My wife wanted me to wear Levi's. She liked their image. I've got a closet filled with reissues she bought me while we were married. After the divorce, I figured I was free to do what I wanted, so I went back to my roots."

I couldn't stifle my grin. "That sounds like something I'd do."

"Don't screw up your marriage, and you won't have to."

We spent the rest of the drive with me telling Loncar about the archives of the Fahrenheit Guild, how they stored both original and dissected versions of garments from history. He interrupted my intel with the occasional clarifying question, but for the most part, he listened, nodded, and drove.

We parked in front of the castle and got out. I led the way to the entrance and yanked on the door. It was the middle of the day, and the door was unlocked. The hallway was dark, but spots of lights spilled out of several rooms, highlighting patches of the Persian rug that lined the hallway. Marguerite poked her head out of one of the rooms.

"Samantha!" she exclaimed. "You've been here so often I should make up a guest bedroom."

"Hi, Marguerite," I said. "This is my friend, Mr. Loncar. He's a denim expert. I brought him here to examine the jeans in the archives."

Her brow furrowed in confusion. "You're too late," she said. "All of the jeans are gone."

32

A WHOLLY DIFFERENT MOTIVE

"What do you mean, 'gone?'" I asked. There was the regular interpretation of "gone" that I was already acquainted with, but I hoped Marguerite could offer me a fresh take on the phrase because my brain didn't want to process what the regular interpretation might mean.

"When I got here this morning, the inventory was missing."

"How well do you know the archives?" I asked. At Marguerite's confused look, I rephrased my question. "There are twenty-five different garments in storage. You must know the inventory well to recognize that two are gone."

"You don't understand," she said. "Hans doesn't have one pair of jeans; he has an entire collection. Close to a hundred pairs."

"You mean the jeans in the study," I said with considerable relief. "I helped Lucy move them to the storage closet after you laundered them."

"Yes, those jeans. They were stored in the wine cellar

until Hans had them moved to the study. He wanted to display them. He said they represented his life's work."

I remembered the piles of jeans in the study, how they'd been strewn upon every available surface. I pictured Hans on the sofa, half-buried under them.

At the time, I thought Jameson was a castle employee, but now I knew he'd been hiding out. And even though Hans was now dead, his killer was still out there, and until that person was caught, Jameson wasn't safe. I understood why Dante felt the need to get Jameson out of town so quickly.

My sense of unease rose as I considered what Marguerite said. There was no way to ask more questions without cluing her into my suspicions, and if she remained one of the people with a master key who had the run of the place, I couldn't discount the fact that she might not be as beyond suspicion as I'd originally thought.

"I'd like to take Mr. Loncar to the archives," I said to Marguerite. I modulated my voice and leaned into the notion that I was a fashion expert—which, as it turned out, was the one thing about me that had never ceased to be true. "As a consultant, I think he'd appreciate knowing the conditions the guild used to preserve the historical garments."

If Marguerite were guilty of something, she did a good job of hiding it. "Go on up," she said lightly.

It never occurred to me that the piles of jeans I'd seen in the study were of value, but if they documented seventy-seven years of denim history, then—I did some quick math based on the prices I'd found online during my research last night—the value of the jeans in that room would have been over a million dollars.

A million dollars!

Stealing that inventory presented a wholly different motive that had nothing to do with the crimes Hans committed.

There was nothing worth showing Loncar in the archive room, but I needed a place for us to talk freely. We reached the second floor and I led Loncar around the landing to the room that housed the pattern pieces. I waited until we were inside the room with the door shut to talk.

"I failed denim history," I confessed. "My boyfriend at the time, Bowe or Ben or Bill—some B name—worked the projection room at the historic theater off-campus, and I got free admission."

Loncar raised both eyebrows and stared at me. "You don't remember his name?"

"It was college. Do you remember everybody you dated in college?"

It was a rhetorical question, but he responded anyway. "I dated my ex-wife in college," he said. "I wish I could forget her name, but the alimony checks remind me every month."

I was consistently surprised when Loncar shared something personal with me, and this was no different. We'd bonded over denim in the car, and now he related to me as an equal. I could feel it.

"What's your point?" he added, and just like that, we were back to our the way we were.

"Instead of going to class, I watched classic movies." I got lost in my memories for a moment, recalling the week

I saw *Cool Hand Luke* twenty-three times. That was a lot of eggs. "I retook the class pass-fail so I could get the credits without worrying about my grade, and I doubled up on early American designers to boost my GPA."

"And?"

"The night I was here, the night Hans was murdered—I was in the study with all those jeans, and I had no idea they were valuable. I never thought about the historical context of work pants. I had no idea I was being recruited to represent the importance of the original five-pocket jean in fashion history. *You'd* make a better candidate for Hans's position than I would."

Loncar, to his credit, didn't automatically agree. "One could argue that Levi's 501s *are* an essential part of early American fashion. They changed the way men dressed for work and have been around, largely unchanged, for over a hundred years."

I dropped into a chair and put my head in my hands. "I can't believe you know more about this than I do."

Loncar lowered himself into the seat next to me. "How many pairs of jeans would you say were in the study?"

"Over a hundred. They were on the desk and the floor and the sofa. When I found Hans's body, he was partially buried under them."

"There weren't any jeans in the study when we found Jameson," Loncar said.

"They've been moved. But the day I showed Madden the yearbooks, and the day I found the trip mechanism that opened the bookcase. All those jeans were there. You saw them too."

"Those jeans weren't old."

"You heard Marguerite. Hans was sorting through his

archive of samples." I felt a glimmer of hope. "Maybe you don't know as much about jeans as you think you do?"

Loncar glared at me. "The jeans in the study were purchased at local department stores and outlets. They weren't vintage."

"They weren't new, either. They didn't have tags, and the denim was soft. They'd all been washed and showed signs of wear, you know, whiskers at the crotch, a faded square for a wallet, stuff like that."

"Factories can produce jeans that look worn." He glanced at my legs. "Did you break that pair in yourself?"

I held my feet out in front of me and stared at the denim on my legs. The fabric was mid-blue, a shade that was intended to look like I'd had them for decades. The knees were threadbare, and the hem had been frayed. I'd probably worn them twice since I bought them, mostly because I favored dark wash.

"Point taken," I said.

It was hard to believe Loncar could be so sure, but I had to admit I was out of my element. Aside from the jeans I'd inherited from my dad, none of the ones I owned bore the Levi's, Wrangler, or Lee logo. Working at a luxury retailer meant getting a healthy discount, and when you're fed a constant stream of advertising propaganda that tells you which are the must-have brands, you buy in (literally).

Detective Loncar being right altered the entire foundation on which our cooperative relationship had been built. But something, some detail I couldn't quite place, kept me from admitting I was wrong. I'd been accused of being stubborn in the past, and while Loncar had given me every indication that he knew what he was talking about now, I couldn't dismiss my gut feeling about this.

Loncar, perhaps bolstered by the discovery that he'd taken the lead with his unexpected knowledge, kept talking, but I missed most of what he said while kicking myself for choosing a frat boy and free movie admittance over a lecture that could help solve a mystery. But then he said something that caught my attention.

"Can you repeat that?"

Loncar looked embarrassed. "I'll show you what to look for on a pair of true vintage jeans if you want to know. I know the tables are temporarily turned, but fashion is more of your wheelhouse than mine."

And then, the memory I'd been seeking came back to me. "Oh my god," I said. "Oh my god, oh my god, oh my god."

"What?"

"I gave Madden a urine sample," I said. "The night Hans was murdered. I was drugged, and after I found the body, I thought maybe he'd been drugged with the same thing, and I had no idea about metabolism speed, and I peed in the nut jar so Madden could test it."

The confidence of knowledge left Loncar's expression, and in its place was the blank stare of a person who questions every decision that brought them to where they are right now.

"You said you were drugged with a benzodiazepine, right?"

"Flunitrazepam," I supplied.

"That drug takes days to metabolize. The coroner would be able to detect it in Hans's bloodstream in the autopsy."

"Madden told me that too. But Madden's a nice guy, and he took my sample anyway, which is the point. My pee isn't the clue," I said. "The jeans are."

"You lost me."

"I was embarrassed about handing Madden a nut jar filled with," I made a face, "you know, so I wrapped the jar in a pair of jeans and stuffed them into a bag from the trash."

I grabbed Loncar's arm and leaned forward. "The jeans that were in the study *were* vintage. I'm sure of it. They weren't stolen last night; they were stolen the night Hans was killed. I can't believe I didn't figure it out before now."

"Figure out what?"

"Someone must have stolen the valuable jeans and replaced them before any of us noticed."

33

A MUCH-NEEDED SCANDAL

LONCAR PULLED OUT HIS PHONE. HE PRESSED A NUMBER from his speed dial. "It's Loncar. I understand Ms. Kidd gave you a urine sample the night Mr. Braeburn was murdered. Where is this sample now?" He gave Madden a moment to speak. I strained my ears to hear the answer through the phone, but darn that Loncar if he didn't keep the volume down to prevent casual eavesdropping. "Sure. Okay. Tell her to sit on it until I get there." He hung up.

"Madden gave your urine sample to the coroner. She performed the autopsy and found the drug in Mr. Braeburn's system. The levels were high enough to send him into cardiac arrest, which she determined was the cause of death. Your sample is in a refrigerated evidence locker at the morgue."

"Then the jeans must be there too." I jumped up. "Let's go," I said.

He held up his hands. "Not so fast. I didn't ask Madden about the jeans, so he thinks this is about the toxicology report. I want to see the garment before upending his whole case."

Loncar still didn't believe me. Based on what I'd told him about failing Denim 101, I couldn't blame him. But last night, after sorting my clothes, after logging into eBay to find out the going rate on fashion-by-the-pound, I'd studied. I might not know about jeans the way I knew about shoes, but I knew the jeans I'd helped Lucy pack up at the castle were different from the ones I'd sorted in my tidying spree last night.

"Come on," Loncar said, leaving the archive room. "I'll drop you off on the way."

"That makes no sense. The coroner is in the opposite direction of my house. You'll waste your time." I adjusted my bag over my shoulder. "I'll come with you."

Loncar crossed his arms. "How do you plan to explain your presence?"

"It's my pee."

"It's not about the pee." Loncar's face colored.

I thought for a moment. "How about this: you're providing on-the-job training for a possible adjunct investigator position at your new company?"

"No."

"Today is Bring-Your-Stand-In-Daughter-to-Work day?"

"No."

"You're currently being investigated for improper conduct and until your case is decided, you need an impartial female companion with you at all times."

"No."

"Come on, that last one was good." I wiggled my

eyebrows. "It gives you a much-needed scandal. Makes you seem more like a real PI."

Loncar thought for a moment. "Let me make a phone call first," he said. He pulled out his phone but got into the car before using it. I stood out front and watched him. I'd been stranded at the castle once, and I wasn't about to let it happen a second time.

IT WAS a twenty-minute drive to the coroner's office. Loncar put on the Grateful Dead, which seemed an ironic choice. The coroner's office was out by the Ribbon Regional Airport. I didn't want to admit it to Loncar, but I was excited about the prospects of going. It wasn't every day you get to meet a real, live coroner, and all things considered, I felt I'd earned it. I tried to hide my enthusiasm. Loncar turned into a parking lot marked by a small white sign that said, "County of Berks Coroner's Office and Records Archives."

"First time here?" Loncar asked.

"Yes."

"Be cool. It's not like backstage passes to a concert."

I glanced at the Grateful Dead CD case. "Well…"

Loncar shook his head.

We entered the building. At Loncar's request, I tamped my curiosity. I was here voluntarily (though if I arrived at the coroner's office *in*voluntarily, there's a good chance I wouldn't have the presence of mind to care), and as far as new experiences go, this one was up there.

The entrance opened onto a large room, not unlike the

bullpen at the newspaper. Desks sat around the perimeter of the room, four in total, equipped with computers and covered with file folders, papers, notes, and personal ephemera. Two of the four desks, the ones on the right side of the room below the windows, appeared to have been cleaned recently and sat unattended. At the end of the room, a woman in a green polo shirt sat next to a wall of massive file cabinets. Loncar walked the length of the room to her desk and I trailed behind, surreptitiously glancing at the poster behind her ("Our day starts when your day ends").

Loncar greeted the woman, ignored the chance to introduce me as his colleague, and said Madden was expecting him. She made a phone call and hung up.

"He's in with Patti," she said. "He'll be right out."

"Can we wait in his office?" I asked.

Loncar grabbed my elbow. "We'll wait in the Bereavement Room," he said sternly. He steered me away from the desk, through the large room, and into a smaller one decorated like a waiting room from 1982.

I shook his hand off my elbow. "What?"

"When I worked for the police department, would you ask to wait in my office if I wasn't around?"

"Of course not. But this is different. I'm with you."

"I'm a private citizen."

"She could have let us wait at one of the desks out there," I said.

"One of those desks is Madden's."

I looked at the door that separated us. "He doesn't have an office?"

"The sheriff has an office. Madden is a detective. He and his colleagues work out of that room."

"Then what's the rest of the building for?"

Before Loncar could answer, a door opened. Madden entered with a thin white woman with messy black hair. She wore a black dress shirt and low-slung black trousers. I liked to assess people by their shoes, but hers were covered in little paper booties.

Madden nodded at us and offered an introduction to the woman. "This is the coroner, Patti. Patti, this is Samantha."

"Hi," I said. I jerked my thumb at Loncar. "I'm with him."

"She's not with me," Loncar said quickly. I turned toward him and saw a red flush climb his neck.

"Hey, Charlie," Patti said to him. She had a small smile on her face. She turned to me and said, "Hey, Sam."

"Hey," I said back.

There appeared to be a dynamic at play that I hadn't expected, and it didn't take years of sleuthing to figure out what was going on. Patti's use of Detective Loncar's first name told me everything I needed to know, and what it didn't, the flush on his face did.

Loncar had a crush on the lady coroner!

I suddenly understood why Loncar had resisted my offer to join him. And instead of feeling like I was helping with an investigation, I felt like a third wheel. As fascinating as a tour of the coroner's office might be, I put aside my interest and tried to think up an excuse to leave them alone.

I turned to Loncar. "Give me your keys," I said. I held my hand out. He looked at my hand first, and then at me. "I think I know what was making that rattling sound under your hood." I winked.

Come on, Loncar. Get with the program.

Loncar reached into his jacket pocket. He pulled out his keys and stared at them for a moment. The idea of trusting me with his car appeared to give him pause.

I reached out and grabbed them. "Take your time. I'll wait outside." I pocketed his keys and turned away from the group.

I got all the way to the door when a female voice called out behind me. "Sam, wait up." I turned around and saw Patti coming toward me. "I need to talk to you."

"Me?"

"Yeah, you." She caught up and leaned against the door. It opened onto the cool October air. She passed me and I turned around to see Madden and Loncar staring as the door closed behind me.

34

HIGH STRUNG

"It's not what you think," I said to Patti. "I'm helping Detective Loncar with a case. He normally doesn't use me in the field, but I bribed him today." I held my hands up. "That's it."

"This isn't about that." She put the tips of her fingers into the back pockets of her trousers. Her pants rode down a little and I saw a sliver of her skin through the open buttons on the bottom of her shirt. "It's about your pee."

"That's why we're here!" I exclaimed and then realized how that might sound, especially since I'd told her I'd bribed Loncar to bring me along.

"You're kinda high strung, aren't you?"

"Not usually," I lied. I remembered that Patti was the person who'd told Madden my news, so I spoke freely. "It must be the pregnancy hormones." I put my hand on my abdomen and felt for movement. I should read a blog or something to understand what was about to happen to my body.

"You're not pregnant," she said.

"It's okay," I said. "Madden told me you found out after you ran the toxicology report. I'm not mad. It's an unusual way to find out, sure, but—"

"You're not pregnant," she said again. She paused awkwardly, and then put her hand on her abdomen. "I am."

We stood there like that for a long moment, mirror images of women who'd received the same news and weren't sure exactly how we felt about it. But my news had turned into non-news, which confused my emotional processing center. I dropped my hand to my side.

"I don't understand," I said.

"I didn't test your pee. I tested mine. The night Hans Braeburn came in, Madden put your sample in the evidence refrigerator. I asked him about it the next day, and he said to dispose of it."

By this point, I was more curious than offended. Equating "dispose of it" with "run a pregnancy test on it" was the sort of thing I might have done back when I made irrational decisions lacking any roots in common sense, and I felt I'd found a kindred spirit.

"The tox report showed the presence of the pregnancy hormone. Madden saw the tox reports and assumed the female one was yours."

"You told him I was pregnant."

"Technically, no. I didn't tell him. I ran the tests and when Madden saw the report, he jumped to the conclusion that I tested your sample."

"It's not like Madden to jump to conclusions."

"I may have entered your name into the computer."

She had a defensive stance, as if she thought I expected an apology but saw no reason to provide one.

"Sure," I said, following her train of thought. "You work here. You didn't want anyone to know the pregnancy test was for you."

"Right."

"Still, you couldn't have bought a pregnancy test at the drug store like everyone else?"

She waved her hand toward the building. "This isn't exactly a typical job for a woman. I'm new, and I'm still getting a handle on the tests and equipment. I asked every person who works here to give me a urine sample so I can get practice. Most of them thought I was kidding." At least she had the good sense to look apologetic. "I didn't know you and Madden were close enough that he'd tell you. I didn't think anybody would find out."

I'm sure there were questions I should have asked—how she found out I knew, if she told Madden the truth, if it were ethical for her to use city resources to take a pregnancy test during working hours, and more, but I didn't think of any of them at that moment. All I could think was that the one thing I thought I knew, the thing that scared me and excited me and would have changed my life irrevocably, wasn't true.

"I'm not pregnant," I said, mostly to myself.

"You're not pregnant," Patti repeated. "After Madden told me he told you, I left you a message."

I remembered seeing an unfamiliar number and ignoring it. "I thought that was spam." It was an insignificant response considering the reason she'd been calling, but hindsight is 20/20, and I admit I wasn't thinking clearly. "Does anybody know about you?" I asked, pointing at her.

"No," she said. "I wanted to talk to you first." She turned her head and stared at the building, not speaking for a stretch. "I should probably tell the father next. Depending on that conversation, people here will find out soon enough."

I got the feeling the father was someone she worked with, which could have hinted at office scandal. But she was a coroner, and who wants to have sex on an autopsy table?

As I said, I wasn't thinking clearly.

The door to the building opened and Madden exited with Loncar close behind. Loncar held the familiar plastic grocery store bag.

"Is that them?" I asked.

Loncar nodded. He reached inside the bag and pulled out a pair of faded jeans. There was nothing about them that would have made me look twice. "Are they valuable?"

"Standard Levi's 501. Produced in Vietnam this year. Probably sold for about thirty dollars."

The whole point of me dragging Loncar out here was the belief—the hope—that the jeans I picked up the night I was drugged were somehow related to the case, and I took no consolation in the fact that they were as generic as the ones I'd folded with Lucy.

"They're worthless," I said.

"They're priceless," Madden countered. He took the bag from Loncar and pulled the jeans out. Inside the waistband was the name "R. Weaver." "I'll need a DNA workup to be sure, but I'd bet these are the jeans Jameson's friend was wearing the night he went missing."

35

MY MOST BENT LOGIC YET

HE DROPPED THE JEANS BACK INTO THE BAG AND HANDED IT to Patti. "Get these to the DNA lab."

Patti took the bag and nodded. She glanced back at me. "Are we good?" she asked.

I nodded. This woman had been responsible for the most earth-shattering news I'd received in the past year, and she'd been responsible for canceling it out. Yet I couldn't be angry with her. She knew nothing about me, about Nick, about our ongoing discussions. She didn't know she'd ever meet me face to face or that she'd have to tell me I was in the same state I'd been in a week ago before a rollercoaster of emotions had rocked my world. She'd done something she thought no one would ever know she'd done, and because one person knew, her actions hadn't remained secret.

Loncar, Madden, and I stood in an awkward triangulation, each watching Patti walk away. I didn't know what the two of them were thinking, but I was confident their thoughts weren't the same as mine. Madden was probably wondering how long it would take to get those DNA results, and Loncar—well, he was probably admiring the view.

"So, what's next?" I asked, looking back and forth between their faces. I turned to Madden. "You have your proof. You don't even have to bring Jameson into it. Should we go back to the castle and check the jeans in storage for other identifying marks? No, wait. I helped fold those jeans, and I'm sure they were new. Maybe we requisition Hans's credit card records to see when he bought the new inventory, see if we can line it up with some unsolved cases—"

"The case against Mr. Braeburn is being investigated by the Philadelphia police," Madden said. "If you're right about those jeans—"

"I'm right about those jeans, and you know it," I interjected.

Madden continued as if I hadn't spoken. "If you're right about those jeans, then they'll have what they need to make a public statement about the crimes. Mr. Braeburn is deceased and no longer a threat. Case closed."

"But what about him?" I asked. "He'll get away with it."

"Ms. Kidd," Loncar said.

"Don't 'Ms. Kidd' me," I said, turning on him. "I know he's dead. But there's no justice in this case. I don't even care who killed Hans Braeburn, and I never say things like that."

Detectives Loncar and Madden looked at each other but neither spoke. My frustration was magnified by my conversation with Patti. I turned to Loncar. "Talk about whatever you need to talk about. I'll wait in the car."

I stormed away from them and unlocked Loncar's car. I dropped into the black leather seat and sulked.

I wasn't going to cry. I wasn't. Not here, not now. I was strong and tough and could hold it together until I got into the privacy of my home.

A renegade tear that wasn't paying attention leaked out of my left eye and ran down my cheek. Another one followed. I swiped at them both, and they replenished themselves. I tipped my head back and blinked rapidly and cursed the instincts that demanded I ride along with Loncar. If I'd never gotten into this car, I still wouldn't know.

It was, possibly, my most bent logic yet.

Loncar joined me a few minutes after I got the tears under control. I stared out the passenger-side window and didn't speak. He drove two miles in silence.

"What were you and Patti talking about?" he asked.

"Nothing," I said. In a way, it was the truth.

"Did she say anything about—um, anybody you know?"

"No," I said.

"Are you okay?" he asked. I shrugged. "You're not normally this quiet."

"I've got nothing to say."

"You don't normally have nothing to say."

I didn't say anything to that either.

Loncar and my familiar dynamic was now flipped. The longer we sat there not talking, the more I needed to say out loud the thing I'd just learned, the thing I didn't know how to process, to make it real.

"I thought I was pregnant. I just found out I'm not."

Loncar was a trained investigator, so I imagined he

was running facts through his mind, deducing how a highly anticipated trip to the coroner's office had led to that news.

"I peed in the nut jar, remember? Madden told me Patti tested it and found the pregnancy hormone, but the results were mixed up."

"With whose?"

"Hers."

"Why would she pee in a nut jar?"

I turned toward him. "Is this how our conversations usually sound to you?"

"A little."

After another stretch of silence, Loncar spoke. "I'm going back to the castle. I'd like to take another look at the jeans you put in storage. Do you want me to drop you off or come along?"

It was a pity invitation, but I took it anyway.

We were both quiet for the duration of the drive. Loncar parked out front. "I'm sorry things didn't work out the way you wanted."

"I don't know what I wanted. Can you believe that? After all these years, I still don't know. I've tried resolutions, mantras, podcasts, self-help books, positive affirmations, and even a life coach. I spent last night tidying up my whole house. And I'm no closer to knowing what I want. That's the real problem here. If I can't figure out what I want, then how am I going to be happy? How is Nick going to be happy with me?"

"Maybe you already have what you want," he said. "Maybe you're afraid if you're happy, then life doesn't get better than it is."

"Does it?"

"You never know what's around the corner," he said. "Don't worry so much. Sit back and enjoy the ride."

We entered the castle. Here, in my hometown, was a historical property filled with family heirlooms—or spoils of war. As a private residence, Hans had kept the outside world from knowing what he had in here, and if any of this had been acquired illegally, it would remain his secret.

"It's disturbing, yes?" asked a soft voice behind me. I turned and saw Ahn. Her glossy black hair fit her skull like a cap, perfectly styled and framing her delicate features. She wore a faint amount of eye shadow and dark purple lips that contrasted with teeth so white she must never drink coffee. She reached her hand forward and pointed to a small, curved metal item in the display case. "It's a Samurai sword in its sheath. Dates to the eighteenth century. After the war, Japanese nobility was forced to hand over all weapons to the Allies. Some have never been returned to their rightful owners."

"Is it rare?"

"Sadly, no. More and more surface every day."

"Do you know the history of the one in this case?"

"I saw it the first time I came to the castle. Hans claimed it was a gift from a friend, but I never believed him." She shook her head. "There are two types of people who display war memorabilia. Historians who recognize artifacts as evidence of war crimes and the others. Those who supported the war itself."

Everything I'd learned about Hans said he was the second type, but I got the feeling Ahn didn't need to hear my theory to come to that conclusion.

"What is going to become of the guild?" I asked.

"We will continue to do the work we do. Each of us believes that by memorizing a pattern that represents an important moment in fashion history, we are contributing to a worthwhile movement. Losing access to the castle won't change that."

"You think Lucy will make you meet elsewhere?"

"Lucy?"

"Lucy. Brooks Brothers shirt. She stands to inherit everything, doesn't she?"

Ahn stood even straighter than she had initially. Her stance was almost regal. Nothing about her indicated she hadn't known Lucy's identity, but the lack of reaction felt significant too.

"I did not know her inheritance was public," she said.

Shoot. Lucy hadn't been the one to tell me; Madden had. "It isn't," I said quickly. "I overheard someone talking about it."

Ahn's shoulders relaxed a tiny bit. She looked directly at me. "Best not to repeat that which we learn by improper channels."

"You're right," I said. "Forgive me."

"It is not I whose secret you violated." She smiled sweetly.

There was that word again: *secret.*

Two separate times information that should have been secret had spilled out and changed things. I didn't doubt it would happen again and again and again. Secrets couldn't be kept secret. There was always someone around who could put two and two together. I'd been so willing to believe that Hans had almost gotten away with his horrible crimes that I hadn't seen the one truth to all of it:

he hadn't. His secret was so awful that whoever had killed him had done the world a favor.

"Why are you here?" I asked Ahn. At her curious expression, I added, "I was under the impression the castle was only open for guild meetings. Is there an event today?"

"Yes," she said. "Lucy called an emergency meeting to discuss unfinished business."

She glanced past me, and I looked over my shoulder. Lucy stood at the end of the hallway in front of the closed clubroom door. "It is fortuitous that you are here," Ahn added.

"Me?" The word squeaked out. I put both hands up. "I didn't do anything."

I hadn't heard Lucy's footsteps down the hall, so when she spoke directly behind me, I jumped. "Come with us, Samantha. We'll pick up where we left off."

"But I'm not a member," I said. "Ahn said you were meeting to discuss unfinished business."

"That's right. That unfinished business is you."

WHO KILLED HANS

WITH LUCY IN FRONT OF ME AND AHN BEHIND ME, WE made a short procession down the hall. If scrappy determination was the deciding factor, I could have probably taken either one in a fight, but I had trouble getting a read on them and I couldn't tell if I was the one in danger. Besides, if it turned out one of them was a murderer, then the other would need my help.

I needed to keep working on that unsolicited help thing.

We reached the clubroom and Lucy put her hand on the door. It eased open. Inside, Buck and Cecile sat in leather wingback chairs. Additional seating had been scattered about, giving the room a much more comfortable feel than it had had the night I'd been drugged. A fire burned in the fireplace, and a tray of water glasses and a pitcher coated in condensation sat on the table.

"Surprise," I said, followed by a nervous laugh. "I'm here."

Cecile rose. "Samantha," she said. "We were just discussing you."

"That's what Ahn said." My heart was pounding, though aside from a slight change in seating arrangements and a drastically underwhelming outfit, little had changed from the night I came here for my interview.

"If memory serves, my interview ended right after I gave you my background."

Buck spoke up, "No. It ended right after you told us if we made you a member, you wouldn't be caught dead in jeans." His eyes shifted from my face to my legs, currently clad in designer denim that, according to Detective Loncar wasn't worth the thread used to stitch them together. "Care to amend that statement?"

"I'd like to keep believing it's true."

I stood in front of the four of them. Four people who may never have come together for any other reason, but who collectively honored a field of the arts that the art patrons themselves often overlooked.

Lucy, the inheritor of Hans Braeburn's estate.

Buck, the legacy member with fourth-generation wealth.

Cecile, the international client officer for a bank who stepped in as guild president after Hans's murder.

And Ahn, the quiet Japanese woman with the cultural ties to the same war that Hans had fought in.

None of them seemed scared to be with the others. None of them appeared to have any concern for his or her safety, for the prospect of returning to the castle, or for the fact that Hans's murderer had yet to be caught. They were sitting in a group, discussing my potential membership as if it were business as usual.

Because to them, it was.

And that's when I knew, beyond a shadow of a doubt, who was responsible for the murder of Hans Braeburn.

I scanned their faces. They watched me, waiting for me to speak. A sense of calm came over me, for no reason other than I knew the truth.

"I'm one of you," I said. "I care about clothes, the history of clothes, and the contribution of wardrobe to the world. I'm aware that most people dismiss it as a superficial pursuit and would prefer to buy cheap clothes that add to landfills and perpetuate child labor and untenable work conditions. Like each of you, I get that a thousand-dollar jacket that lasts twenty years is better for the planet than a fifty-dollar jacket that has to be replaced every year. I know we live in a disposable culture, and I know environmentalists don't talk about fashion's role in their equation."

I stopped talking. My mouth was dry, and I would have loved some water, but fool me once and all that. I forced myself to swallow and then continued. "I also love clothes. I love the cut of an A-line skirt with knee-high boots. I love the way hemlines rise and fall in direct proportion to the world's economic state. I love how fashion reflects current events, even when fashion takes inspiration from military sources during wartimes. I love it all."

Lucy settled into an empty leather chair. Ahn remained standing to the right of her. The four of them faced me, judging me. I'd said what I should have said the first night I was here, but based on everything that happened since then, I knew tonight wasn't about fashion history. It was about a different history, and if I didn't confront the issue, I wouldn't make it out alive.

"I know who killed Hans," I said. If I hadn't been watching their faces as closely as they watched mine, I might not have seen the flash in Lucy's eyes, the suppressed grin on Buck's face, and the slight eyebrow drop on Cecile. I might have missed the tightening of Ahn's hand on the back of Lucy's chair. I might not have had the courage to play the one card I had left.

"You each needed to see Hans as a villain because you knew what you—" I looked up and scanned each of their faces, "what you all—had done."

And that was it. One of them wasn't a murderer. All four of them were. "You did it together," I said. "You each played a role in killing Hans Braeburn because you knew that way none of you would go to the police."

I closed my eyes and called back my first night at the castle. When I opened my eyes, I pieced it together. "The drugged water. It wasn't a mistake. You had to drug me so I wouldn't be a reliable witness. But how—how did you know I'd drink the water?"

Four faces stared at me. Four faces that showed no anger, no fear, no hostility. I'd accused them of killing someone and in my experience, that usually nets a denial. But none of them denied it. I was square in the middle of a fashionable Agatha Christie plot, with a cast of suspects who seemed to dislike the victim enough that nobody cared whodunit.

The door to the clubroom eased open and I turned, expecting to see Loncar. But it was Marguerite, the maid. She carried in a fresh pitcher of water and replaced the one that was there. She glanced at me, and then at the others.

"She knows," Cecile said.

Marguerite froze. My mind whirred into motion. Marguerite? Of course! She'd been in on it too. That was the missing piece, how they ensured the drug was delivered to two specific people.

Marguerite stood there, inches from me, holding a heavy glass pitcher. Unlike the others, she looked scared, and that scared me. With one panicked gesture, she could smash the pitcher on the table and use the sharp edges as a weapon. A memory of a similar situation flashed back to me: blood and death and fear in a small office in the department store where I thought I'd be working, the job I thought would be the bridge between my past and my future. So much had happened since then. I couldn't have predicted any of it, and what scared me the most was that I might not be around to see what would happen next.

THE WILDCARD

"YOU ALL PLAYED YOUR ROLES TO PERFECTION," I SAID. "But you each gave yourselves away. Buck," I said, "you became a member when a childhood friend offered you his spot. Where did you say you met him?"

"Camp." He had nothing to hide, and his confidence said as much.

"Youth camp?" I asked. Buck nodded. "Was Hans one of the counselors?" Buck nodded again. This time his expression darkened, as if those childhood memories were corners he'd rather not revisit.

I turned to Ahn. "The Samurai sword in the case out front. How long did it take you to trace it to this castle?"

She bowed her head again, not answering, but not refuting that there was truth to my question.

"And Lucy, your story doesn't quite match up with the one that ran in the newspaper archives. Your grand-mother didn't choose to have an affair with Hans, did she?"

"He raped her," she said.

"You knew the truth when he came to find you, didn't you? You knew all along he was lying."

Lucy didn't have to answer any more of my questions; the truth was plain to see.

I turned to Cecile. "You said you've known Hans forever. How long *is* forever? Long enough to have proof about who he was and what he'd done?"

Cecile stepped forward. "Hans was a murderer before he moved to the states. My family died when his unit moved through Vichy. My parents were part of the French Resistance. I got out and thought I would never see such evil again. The first time he came into the bank to open an account, it was as if I were looking at the devil."

I turned to Marguerite. "And you?"

The maid spoke in a quiet voice. "Three weeks ago, I saw Hans dispose of a body," she said. "He threatened to kill my husband if I said anything to the police."

Three weeks ago. One week before the invitation to join the Fahrenheit Guild had arrived at my house.

Each person in this room had been sitting on their hatred for Hans. He hit the ignition switch when he kidnapped and murdered Regan Weaver. Marguerite didn't have to admit that she'd told one—or all—of the members in this room what had happened. It was an easily deducted conclusion, considering what I knew now.

"What happened to his archives?" I asked. "The real jeans. The valuable ones. They were in the study the night of my interview, but someone swapped them out later. Who has them now?"

The five of them exchanged glances, nodded at Cecile,

and she spoke. "A board member who wishes to remain anonymous purchased the collection for a seven-figure sum."

Lucy spoke up. "It didn't seem right for us to profit from Hans's crimes, so the money was donated to a Philadelphia school for underprivileged boys."

Again, I found myself studying each of their faces, filling in gaps they left open. If the five people in front of me were the only ones to know the truth, then the anonymous member was one of them. When I got to Buck, I hesitated. He offered me the tiniest hint of a smile and a nod, enough to confirm my suspicion that the money had come from him.

"And what about the jeans? Were they donated too?"

"It would have been impossible to separate the jeans from the crimes Hans committed to acquire them," Cecile added. "We can't allow him a legacy, not based on what he did, and we can't risk the questions that would come from people learning of the collection."

I thought back to the day I came back to the castle. I'd been here with Loncar and Dante. I'd helped Lucy move the laundered inventory to the baker's racks in the hallway storage. But that was just it. The jeans we moved weren't the ones I'd seen the night of my interview.

"The jeans are gone," I surmised. "Where?"

"Destroyed," Buck said. "Just like the book Hans named the guild after."

The guild's purported mission was to memorize classic fashion patterns to preserve them for the future, but this garment's history had gotten muddied. Donating them to a museum, selling them to a collector, even giving them away, would have kept Hans's legacy alive. Despite their passion, the people in front of me had been motivated by something bigger than fashion history. I couldn't fault them for their decision.

But still. A million dollars' worth of jeans, a full timeline of denim styles from 1944 to now, gone. Up in flames.

I kept my eyes on Buck. The rest of the group trusted him, but a part of me would always wonder if this were like an Indiana Jones movie instead, where Hans's ill-gotten denim stash had not been destroyed but now resided in one of Buck's dark corners.

Lucy stood and moved toward us. She eased the pitcher out of Marguerite's grip and turned, handing it to Ahn, who set it on the mantle over the fireplace.

"Hans was a bad man," Lucy said. "We each learned that. And now you know it too. The question that matters right now is yours to answer." Lucy looked up at me. "You said you're one of us. Are you willing to prove it?"

The four remaining members of the board, along with Marguerite, waited for my answer. It was what I'd wanted so much a mere week ago: for this group to accept me as one of their own. I'd dressed to impress them, that very first night, and here it was left to me to answer that question. The room went silent. Lucy's question hung in the air. How willing was I to prove I was one of them?

I didn't have to think about it for long. I excused myself and went in search of Detective Loncar and helped him collect evidence to close the case. It would have surprised most people to learn that the case in question wasn't the one we'd spent so much time discussing.

CARL BROKE the story the next day. He reported the time-line of murders Hans Braeburn had committed, starting in 1944, the year he came to the United States, and continuing until this year, his final murder being Regan Weaver. Seventy-seven years of murders. He took the jeans from the victims as a trophy, archiving the significant pairs and hiding the rest in plain sight.

As for his cause of death, it was declared a heart attack. Loncar and Madden had a conversation to which I was not privy, and the case was closed shortly thereafter. Those of us who knew about the benzodiazepines kept quiet. Patti disposed of my urine sample, and Hans's body was cremated.

It was the most unusual case I'd been involved with to date, and I wondered if this signified a bigger shift to a world of people who increasingly felt justified taking matters into their own hands.

I could have spent days, weeks, months wondering about the plan to murder Hans Braeburn, and my role: the wildcard. The unrelated element that made all others have a reason for existing as a group. They'd counted on me; they'd counted on my questions and investigation. Everything from me being poisoned and passing out to me nosing around had been expected, and they'd done their best to keep me spinning on tangents that led nowhere.

I should have been flattered.

What they hadn't counted on was the presence of Jameson. They never could have anticipated a brave, four-teen-year-old boy following Hans from Philadelphia to Ribbon, caught up in circumstances that were more dangerous than he'd ever imagined. They also hadn't counted on me asking for help and relying on my network to get at the truth.

I broke the news—*our news*—to Nick. Unlike the confrontation with the guild board members at Braeburn Castle, this was a quiet moment shared between two people who had managed to keep our non-news to ourselves. They say you can't lose what you never had, but we felt the loss anyway. We had to move on. At least I knew we'd move on together.

By the time the Ribbon newspapers had been read and recycled, I'd carted twenty-five reinforced garbage bags of clothes to a local women's shelter. Those bags were my past. They were dates I'd had, promotions I'd received, trips I'd taken, and in a few cases, experiences I'd rather forget.

But to embrace the future, I had to make space. Loncar was right; I didn't know what was around the corner. But whatever it was, I wanted to be ready.

On my way home from the shelter, I slowed for a yellow light. A red Mustang pulled up alongside me and the driver rolled the window down. I could tell from the look on his face he wanted to race.

"That your car?" he asked.

"Yep."

"Limited edition, right?"

"Yep."

"You happy with the performance?"

"Yep."

He revved his engine. "You want to test the acceleration?"

"No, thank you," I said. "I don't care that much about the performance. I bought it because it was pretty."

The light changed, and the Mustang left me in his dust. For the first time in a long time, I wasn't in a hurry. I was happy exactly where I was.

WANT MORE SAMANTHA? Preorder Stark Raving Mod, Samantha Kidd Mystery #13, coming June 2022!

ABOUT

National bestselling author Diane Vallere writes funny and fashionable character-based mysteries. After two decades working for a top luxury retailer, she traded fashion accessories for accessories to murder. A past president of Sisters in Crime, Diane started her own detective agency at age ten and has maintained a passion for shoes, clues, and clothes ever since. Find out more at dianevallere.com.

Want a bonus book? Sign up for Diane's Weekly DiVa Club and receive BONBONS FOR YOUR BRAIN, a collection of insightful essays designed to make you laugh, think, and feel less alone. Subscribe at dianevallere.com/weekly-diva.

ACKNOWLEDGMENTS

Thank you for reading Samantha Kidd's latest killer fashion adventure. I've always known Samantha will take me to places I didn't expect to go, and this book was no exception.

As someone who gave up jeans from 2005-2019, I knew a book focused on them would require a deep dive on denim. Twelve pairs purchased, seven pairs kept, and hundreds examined and I can say what is included here is the tip of the iceberg. Special thanks to Heddels.com, who (unknowingly) became my go-to resource for all things denim, and to Levi Strauss for producing the famous five-pocket jean in 1873 and keeping up the good work ever since.

When I first considered the personal-growth aspect of Samantha's emotional journey, I thought it might be fun to take a fashion-obsessed character with overflowing closets and have her read *The Life-Changing Magic of Tidying Up*. I read the book to find humorous ways to incorporate it into Samantha's mindset. Little did I realize the impact it would have on both of us!

I didn't set out to write a book about a Nazi, though sometimes when bad guys walk on stage they're difficult to ignore. Information about this aspect of the book came through a variety of channels, with specific thanks to History Today, for the information about fashion and the Third Reich, and Gizmodo for the article about Nazi summer youth camps across the country in the 1930s.

Thank you to the coroner's offices in Santa Barbara, CA and Ramsey County, Minnesota, for having YouTube video tours of your facilities. You never know who's watching!

As always, this book was not a solo mission. Thank you to Gigi Pandian, Lisa Matthews, and Ellen Byron for our weekly brainstorming sessions, Jordaina Sydney Robinson for helping me work out the emotional stuff, Marie Kondo for your passion for tidying up, Amy Ross Jolly for your insightful comments on the early manuscript, the Polyester Posse for helping to spread the word, and subscribers of the Weekly DiVa for being in my orbit.

Lastly, to my family. I love you all.

Apprehend Me No Flowers

Teacher's Threat

The Kill of it All

Made in the USA
Middletown, DE
13 November 2021

51607402R00163